WILLIAM SHAKESPEARE

*

THE COMEDY OF
ERRORS

EDITED BY
STANLEY WELLS

PENGUIN BOOKS

Penguin Books Ltd, Harmondsworth, Middlesex, England
Penguin Books, 625 Madison Avenue, New York, New York 10022, U.S.A.
Penguin Books Australia Ltd, Ringwood, Victoria, Australia
Penguin Books Canada Ltd, 2801 John Street, Markham, Ontario, Canada L3R 1B4
Penguin Books (N.Z.) Ltd, 182–190 Wairau Road, Auckland 10, New Zealand

—

This edition first published in Penguin Books 1972
Reprinted 1976, 1980, 1981

—

This edition copyright © Penguin Books, 1972
Introduction and notes copyright © Stanley Wells, 1972

—

Made and printed in Great Britain by
Richard Clay (The Chaucer Press) Ltd,
Bungay, Suffolk
Set in Monotype Ehrhardt

CONTENTS

INTRODUCTION

The Comedy of Errors is Shakespeare's masterpiece, if we use that word to mean the first work in which mastery of a craft is displayed. It is a fully formed work of art, completely successful in its own terms. In craftsmanship it is rivalled among Shakespeare's first eight or nine plays only by *Richard III* and *Love's Labour's Lost*; and *The Comedy of Errors* is more compact, if less ambitious, than either of these. It has nevertheless been held in low critical esteem, accused of being an over-derivative farce scarcely redeemed by any pretensions to literary merit. It has been often performed, but almost always in considerably altered versions. This is basically because it is exceptionally short, the shortest of all Shakespeare's plays. Occasionally it has been made still shorter, so as to fit into a double bill. More commonly it has been lengthened, by the addition of music, song, dance, mime, and extra dialogue. Performers have no doubt been encouraged in their disrespect by the notion that it is a farce, and may therefore be treated more freely than if it were a comedy. The American director Margaret Webster has written: 'It is one of the few plays which may be stylized to the limit of a director's invention and with all the extended artifice of music, ballet, and comedy tricks. So trimmed and graced, and mercilessly cut, it may still serve as an hors d'œuvre for the less sophisticated. . . . The play is not bad vaudeville' (*Shakespeare Today* (1957), page 139). This is one expression of a generally patronizing attitude to the original play as a result of

7

which it has been given little chance to prove itself on the stage.

It would be wrong to write of *The Comedy of Errors* as if it were one of Shakespeare's greatest comedies. It lacks the range, the variety, the subtlety, the richness of plays that he was soon to compose. But it would also be wrong to write of it as if it were not both the most brilliant comedy that had so far been written in English, and also – lest this imply merely relative success – a completely assured work for which no excuses need be made. On the rare occasions when it has been played more or less as it was written, it has demonstrated its capacity to entertain, in the fullest sense of the word. A play does not retain this capacity for close on four hundred years if it is merely – as this play's detractors have implied – a slick piece of theatrical mechanism.

Criticism of the play has been bedevilled especially by the question of whether it is a farce or a comedy, and by the assumption that farce is less respectable than comedy. To distinguish between the kinds is often not easy. No one would dispute that, for example, Feydeau's *A Flea in her Ear* is clearly a farce, and that *Twelfth Night* is equally clearly a comedy. But many comedies, including *Twelfth Night*, sometimes approach the condition of farce. Characteristics of farce, it is generally agreed, include absurdities of plot, stylization of action, subordination of character to plot, and a dissociation of response in which violence evokes laughter rather than pity. All these characteristics are present in *Twelfth Night*, though this play also has features such as romance, depth of characterization, tenderness of emotion, and comparative concern for credibility, which weight it heavily on the side of comedy. Only when farcical characteristics outweigh comic ones is a play felt to be a farce rather than a comedy; and finally, of course, there is no meter by which relative quantities can be judged. *The Comedy of Errors* certainly has some of the characteristics of farce, and to a greater degree than has *Twelfth Night* (to which nevertheless it is closely related). Characterization is generally slight: but it is not negligible; the action is improbable: but it has its own logic; there is a crescendo of violence, working through a series of beatings to a climax on stage in the scene (IV.4) in which Antipholus of Ephesus and his Dromio are bound: but the most violent episode of the action is narrated (V.1.169–83), not shown. There are, too, many humanizing episodes which count in the scale against a purely farcical classification. Real suffering is expressed by several characters, especially Egeon, who (like Antonio in *Twelfth Night*) provides a centre of emotional gravity; the plot touches on serious issues which are developed in the dialogue; the action, though generally speedy, relaxes from time to time to accommodate reflective and romantic sentiments; there is a corrective element in the comedy; and the play ends, not in the chaos characteristic of some types of farce, but in a re-establishment of order and harmony, accompanied by an assertion and demonstration of humane values, such as are associated with the most romantic of romantic comedies.

If, then, *The Comedy of Errors* is a farce, it is so by such a narrow margin that it is by no means a typical specimen. To pigeonhole it seems pointless. It is a play in which Shakespeare draws on a variety of literary and dramatic traditions, with characteristic eclecticism; and it deserves to be considered in its own right.

*

Of the circumstances in which it was composed and first acted, we know little. The most interesting piece of

information we have comes from an account of the
Christmas revels held in 1594 at Gray's Inn, London.
They began on 20 December and continued well into the
New Year. On the night of 28 December a special performance of some unspecified kind was planned, but so
many people were present, and revelry reached such a
height, that 'there arose such a disordered tumult and
crowd upon the stage that there was no opportunity to
effect that which was intended.' Eventually 'it was
thought good not to offer anything of account saving
dancing and revelling with gentlewomen; and after such
sports a comedy of errors (like to Plautus his *Menaechmus*)
was played by the players. So that night was begun, and
continued to the end, in nothing but confusion and
errors; whereupon it was ever afterwards called "The
Night of Errors".'

Shakespeare's play, of course, is based on *Menaechmi*,
and it seems quite likely that the play given on this
occasion was his. Other details in the account of the revels
support the identification. But there is a major problem.
Shakespeare's play had not appeared in print, so it is
unlikely to have been played by any company other than
that to which he belonged, the Lord Chamberlain's Men.
But they were paid for a performance at the Court, at
Greenwich, on 28 December, and also on 26 December.
However, the accounts for Court performances also show
a payment to another company on 28 December; so it
may be that the records are mistaken, and that the
Chamberlain's Men actually played at Court on 26 and
27 December and at Gray's Inn on the following day.

If the play presented at Gray's Inn was Shakespeare's,
was this its first performance? Its shortness might suggest
that it was written for a special occasion. But the only
honest answer to the question is 'We do not know.'

Nor do we know precisely when it was written. There are a few topical and literary allusions and echoes (noted in the Commentary to this edition), but all are inconclusive. Some people have believed that this is Shakespeare's first play; but it is difficult to see how so masterly a display of theatrical craftsmanship could precede *The Two Gentlemen of Verona*, which is a much less accomplished play even though its poetic style seems more closely related to that of Shakespeare's maturity. At the same time, 1594 seems a little late on stylistic grounds, since it would bring the play very close to *A Midsummer Night's Dream*, *Romeo and Juliet*, and *The Merchant of Venice*. The best we can say is that it probably belongs to the early 1590s.

Looking at *The Comedy of Errors* in the light of Shakespeare's later work, we may easily see it as an experimental piece in which he submitted himself more thoroughly to a dominant influence – here, that of Roman comedy and its English adaptations – than he was later to do. But the experiment of adapting Roman drama to native conventions was not new, and had in fact produced some of the more successful English plays of the previous three or four decades. Latin was the ordinary medium of education in the grammar schools, and the comedies of Plautus and Terence were popular in schools, both because their language was not too difficult and because of their power to entertain. Shakespeare must have studied some of them when he was a boy. If it is true that he was once 'a schoolmaster in the country', he may have taught some of them to his pupils. He must have seen some of them acted, whether in the original or in English translation. And he is also likely to have known earlier adaptations of Roman matter and technique into English, such as Nicholas Udall's *Ralph Roister Doister*, written in mid-century for the boys of Eton College, and *Gammer*

Gurton's Needle, a play of uncertain authorship performed about 1553 at Christ's College, Cambridge. It is even possible that in *The Comedy of Errors* he was so conscious of working within a tradition that he deliberately adopted a somewhat archaic style in deference to what he regarded as its established conventions.

This play may seem less mature in literary style than in dramatic craftsmanship; but it does not lack stylistic variety. Shakespeare uses a number of verse forms, and shows a full sense of their varied possibilities and of their dramatic fitness. The norm is, as usual, blank verse, as in the first scene, where it is interspersed with occasional couplets and reveals great skill in the construction of long narrative verse paragraphs. A very different use of the same form is demonstrated by Dromio of Ephesus's opening speech (I.2.43–52; see page 21 below). There are some extended passages of couplets, as in Act II, scene 1, between Adriana and Luciana, where they point the formal quality of the sisters' disputation, and in the following scene, where they serve first to set off Antipholus's bemusement. The Dromios sometimes speak blank verse, but at other times their presence causes the form to alter to prose, or to a rhyming doggerel that Shakespeare must have intended to have an archaic effect. It is associated with the drama of the previous generation, and is used in *Ralph Roister Doister* and *Gammer Gurton's Needle*. Shakespeare's use of it here may exploit its unfashionableness for comic effect. It points the irony, for example, of the disputation on hospitality at the beginning of Act III, scene 1. A more obviously formal measure is that of the quatrain, used mainly for high sentiment, as in Luciana's address to her sister's supposed husband at the beginning of Act III, scene 2, and, more lyrically, in his romantic response. The style of the play reveals an extensive employment of the devices studied and practised by the rhetoricians of the time.

The verse is always competent, and sometimes rises to brilliance, as in the lyrical power of Antipholus's wooing (III.2.29–70), the comic precision of Antipholus of Ephesus's indignant description of Dr Pinch (V.1.237–42), or the genuine if somewhat dated eloquence of Egeon's lament (V.1.308–19). More important still, it is always used with a feeling for dramatic effect. To say that the play lacks detachable set-pieces of poetry is to praise its economy. The prose, too, is constructed with controlled artistry, rising in the description of the kitchen wench (III.2.92–154) to a virtuosic – and splendidly actable – piece of fantasy reminiscent of the best work of Shakespeare's contemporary, Thomas Nashe. Throughout the play Shakespeare seems to have subordinated his verbal powers to an overall purpose which included an element of pastiche of earlier adaptations of Roman comedy, a little perhaps out of a sense of decorum, more for comic effect. If this reflects a deliberate intention, it may help to explain the relative absence from the play of the kind of lyrical verse that Shakespeare seems already to have achieved in *The Two Gentlemen of Verona* and, possibly, *Love's Labour's Lost*, and that we associate with his greatest comedies.

*

There is no question that Shakespeare's main source was Plautus's *Menaechmi*. The first English translation, by William Warner, was not published till 1595. Shakespeare may have seen this in manuscript, but he almost certainly knew the play in Latin. It has a long Prologue (omitted in Warner's translation) telling of twin brothers, one of whom wandered from home as a boy, as a result of which his father died of grief. The boy, Menaechmus, now lives, prosperous and married, in Epidamnus. As the action opens, he has stolen a valuable cloak from his shrewish wife, and goes along with his parasite, Peniculus, to visit his mistress, the courtesan Erotium, to whom he intends to give the cloak. He tells her to prepare dinner for them while they go to do some business in the city. She gives orders to her male cook, Cylindrus. Menaechmus's twin is shown arriving at Epidamnus with his slave in search of his brother. The cook encounters him, and is bewildered not to be recognized. The twin's slave advises him that this is just a courtesan's trick, typical of this disreputable town. Erotium herself then appears, and reveals a bewildering knowledge of the brother's past. The slave suspects she is a witch, but his master decides to pretend to be the man she takes him for, and see what he can get out of it. She asks him to take the cloak to the dyer's to be trimmed and altered, and he agrees that he will do this after dinner.

The parasite thinks his friend has deliberately given him the slip, and gone to dinner without him. He comes upon the visiting twin, who has dined and is on his way to the dyer's. Rebuking him, the parasite is denied, so he decides to go to tell the wife about her husband's disloyal behaviour. Erotium's maid comes to ask the twin to take a chain to the goldsmith's to be altered. It is one that had belonged to Menaechmus's wife. Having thus acquired a valuable cloak and a gold chain, the twin decides to leave while the going is good. We then see the wife and parasite together, lying in wait to take the cloak from the visiting twin before he arrives at the dyer's with it. Her real husband, who has been delayed, enters on his way to visit Erotium. His wife accuses him of the theft of the cloak, but he says he has merely lent it to his mistress, and promises to return it. He asks Erotium for it, but as she believes she has given him both it and the chain, she thinks he is tricking her, and shuts him out of her house.

Now we see his brother again, carrying the cloak and looking for his slave, to whom he has given his purse. The wife meets and accuses him. She calls to her father for help, and asks to be allowed to return home. But he is unsympathetic, suggesting that she has brought her trouble on herself. The twin's responses to her father's questions cause him to be regarded as mad, and he thinks the same of the wife and her father. They threaten to have him carried off. He puts on an act of madness to frighten them away, and then slips off to his ship.

The father returns with a physician, and now the resident Menaechmus enters. Understandably, he resents being treated as a madman. They go to instruct four men to take him by force to the physician's house. Shut out from both his home and his mistress's house, he is at a loss for a refuge. Now his twin's slave enters, telling us how well he has looked after his master's interests. He sees his master, as he thinks, being carried off, and attempts to rescue him. Between them they beat off the porters. The slave demands his freedom as a reward, but of course Menaechmus does not understand him. He resigns himself to the situation, and prepares to act as is expected of him. He goes off to try to get the cloak back from Erotium so that he can make peace with his wife. His exit is immediately followed by the entrance of his twin, abusing the slave, who has encountered him and who demands the freedom he has been promised. Now Menaechmus enters, and for the first time the twins are seen together. The cause of confusion is evident. The brothers are happily reunited, the slave is freed, and the brothers agree to go to live with one another in Syracuse. The one of Epidamnus will sell all his belongings, including his wife, though there is a danger that no one will bid for her.

Anyone who knows *The Comedy of Errors* will recognize from this plot-summary that Shakespeare derived many of his incidents from Plautus. More important is the fact that he added much to his basic source – his play is roughly half as long again – and that he arranged both his derived and his invented elements to create an independent structure of much more ingenious complexity. A description of some of the changes, and a discussion of the possible motives underlying them, may help to demonstrate that Shakespeare's play is less fundamentally derivative than is sometimes supposed.

With the invention of a twin brother for the slave, Shakespeare at one stroke increased greatly the possibilities of comic confusion. In Plautus there is no one whom the visiting brother is likely to take for anyone else, but in Shakespeare he too can be wrong, about the Dromios. In Shakespeare's play every character knows, and may easily encounter, either a twin master or servant or both, and so is liable to error, except the Abbess, who was separated from both her children and from the Dromios when they were infants. As the character least susceptible to error, she is peculiarly fitted to resolve the action. Shakespeare also increases the number of minor characters, adding for instance the Goldsmith, Balthasar, and the Merchants, in order to increase the possibilities of confusion.

In his addition of the twin Dromios, Shakespeare seems to have been influenced by another play of Plautus, *Amphitruo*, of which no English translation is known to have existed. An episode in that play tells how Alcmena was seduced by Jupiter disguised as her husband while Mercury, disguised as her husband's servant, kept the true servant away, then refused admission to the husband himself. This episode obviously influenced Shakespeare's Act III, scene 1, though, characteristically, Shakespeare raises the moral tone by substituting the dinner party of *Menaechmi* for the bedroom setting of *Amphitruo*.

Shakespeare's addition of a twin servant not only increases the opportunities for mistakes of identity but also allows him to create a series of episodes which, if they do not amount to a fully developed sub-plot, at least serve something of this function, causing the Dromios' adventures to counterpoint their masters'. For example, shortly after Antipholus of Syracuse has been claimed by Adriana as her husband, his Dromio suffers from the attentions of the kitchen wench; and in the play's charming *coda* the twin Dromios are given their independent reunion scene.

The invention of the twin Dromios, then, is primarily responsible for the increased intellectual complications of the action. Equally important in the overall design of the play, and especially in its emotional effect, is the enclosing of the main action within the framework of a serious story. *Menaechmi* proceeds to the reunion of twin brothers. Shakespeare increases the potential happiness of his ending not merely by adding a twin servant, but also by working towards the reunion of a man with the son he has been seeking, one he has not been seeking, and with his long-lost wife; and he gives special intensity to the reunions by the fact that they coincide with the hour appointed for this man's execution, and finally cause it to be averted.

There is a seed for this framing story in the statement in Plautus's Prologue to *Menaechmi* that the father died of grief at the apparent loss of one of his sons. In altering and developing this idea Shakespeare drew on a story which he was to use much more fully some fifteen years later, in *Pericles*. This is the story of Apollonius of Tyre, well known to Shakespeare's forebears and contemporaries, partly through the English version in John Gower's *Confessio Amantis*. Shakespeare's borrowings from this story in *The Comedy of Errors* are slight in themselves, and some of them are among the commonplaces of romance literature. The separation of relatives by a storm at sea, subsequent journeyings, and final reunion could be paralleled in many other tales, old and more recent. It is the fact that the separated wife goes into religious life, and does so at Ephesus, that makes us most confident that Shakespeare had this particular story in mind when he wrote *The Comedy of Errors*. Probably this link through plot material helped him to develop the romanticism latent in certain areas of *Menaechmi* and to infuse into the story of mistaken identities an emotional reality and a sense of wonder that are absent from the Roman farce and that we associate more readily with Shakespeare's late tragi-comedies such as *Pericles* and *The Tempest*.

So, while Shakespeare derived much of his material for this play, he retained control over it, altering and complicating his sources as he felt the need. Like many of his contemporaries who translated Italian and French prose fiction into English, he seems to have felt a concern to play down features of the story that might have offended. In *The Comedy of Errors*, for instance, Antipholus of Ephesus does not steal his wife's cloak, as does his counterpart in Plautus. Most likely to cause offence was the easy acceptance in the Roman play of the institution of the courtesan. Here, indeed, Shakespeare had to wrestle with somewhat intransigent material. He reduces the importance of the role. He takes away the lady's name, calling her simply 'Courtesan'. He causes Antipholus of Ephesus to visit her only under extreme provocation, and to claim that his visits do not involve infidelity to his wife; and he makes our belief in this claim fundamental to his characterization of the wife, Adriana. Inevitably there is some strain in this, since the function of a courtesan is generally held to extend beyond the provision of 'excellent discourse' (III.1.109). Actresses are understandably tempted to burlesque the role, playing it as a comic caricature of a more-or-less high-class prostitute; but to do so is to deny Shakespeare's discernible intentions. The Dromios, too, caused him problems, not on moral grounds, but because in the Roman context they have the status of slaves. But even in Latin comedy, slaves often behave in a familiar manner with their masters, and Shakespeare's portrayal of them in the traditionally easy relationship of master and servant, resembling that of Petruchio and Grumio (in *The Taming of the Shrew*), need cause no more than momentary difficulty. On the whole, Shakespeare is remarkably successful in solving the problems imposed by adapting a story dependent on a historical and foreign setting to the tastes and understanding of his audience.

*

From the narrative elements out of which Shakespeare constructed his play, it is worth turning to the dramatic structure itself. In only two of his plays did he show any concern with the neo-classical principle that a play should observe the unities of time, place, and action: a principle propounded by some of the dramatic theoreticians of his own time, and even by some of its playwrights. The two plays are this one, written early in his career, and *The*

Tempest, probably his last non-collaborative play. Both
tell of events that occurred over a period of many years.
This means that, if the unity of time is to be observed,
much background material has to be conveyed. In both
plays Shakespeare chooses the simplest method of doing
this, that is, through a long narrative speech placed early
in the action. It is of course an unrealistic technique,
though in *The Comedy of Errors* Egeon at least has both
an uninformed listener and good reason to tell his story,
whereas in *The Tempest* there seems no special reason
why Prospero should have delayed so long in telling
Miranda about the strange events of her infancy. Shakespeare's implausible expository technique in both plays
has been criticized explicitly and, in *The Comedy of
Errors*, implicitly by performers who have treated Egeon's
narrative derisorily. A sentence or two from Gordon
Crosse's account of Komisarjevsky's Stratford production
of 1938 will illustrate this, as well as providing a remarkably concentrated series of the kinds of misunderstanding
and false logic that have served as an excuse for mal-
treating the play in the theatre: 'The play is a farce; its
purpose, therefore, is to rouse uproarious laughter, and
this the producer did by extravagant but legitimate
methods. The fun began, as the phrase is, from the word
"go"; the crowd guying Aegeon's exposition by their
ridiculous business and interjections' (*Shakespearean
Playgoing 1890–1952* (1953), page 95). And in 1971 *The
Times* reviewed enthusiastically a production at the
Edinburgh Festival in which Egeon was 'brought on as a
condemned British alien who delivers his speech about the
storm to a crowd cowering under umbrellas from the rain
clouds of Auld Reekie' and in which 'the long expository
speeches (always Shakespeare's weak point) are sacrificed'.

Objections to long expository speeches are understandable, especially from critics who have been brought up on naturalistic drama. Shakespeare himself shows a concern to avoid or alleviate them in some of his plays. But experience in the theatre suggests that if they are spoken well enough, and seriously enough, they are capable of enthralling an audience as much as rapid passages of dramatic interchange. Egeon's opening narrative is a sophisticated piece of rhetorical verse. It derives dramatic interest from his immediate situation and from the effect his story makes on his listeners. Its deliberately slow pace sets off the vivacity of the action that is to follow, while its serious matter and tone prepare the audience both to attend to the more serious implications of the body of the play and, above all, to respond adequately to the denouement, when a happy ending to this tale of Egeon's is enacted before us. The very mode of the play might thus be said to move from narrative into drama.

After the adagio opening comes a brief transition episode referring back to it. Antipholus of Syracuse is shown arriving in Ephesus, permitting the actor to create some sympathy for the character, and showing him, too, to be in search of 'a mother and a brother' (I.2.39). But the pace changes to a brisk allegro with the clattering entry of the Ephesian Dromio, whose blank verse, with its end-stopped lines, its largely monosyllabic diction, its rhythmic regularity, and its staccato sound effects (lines 43 onwards), contrasts with the melancholy enjambements and long vowels of Antipholus's lament. Now begins the series of mistaken encounters which make up the body of the play. But Shakespeare does not unleash them upon us all at once. The next scene (II.1) introduces us to Adriana and Luciana engaged in a serious-enough discussion of male–female relationships, establishing Adriana as a somewhat rebellious and impatient character, easily made jealous by Dromio's report of his supposed master's odd behaviour. After this the number of mistaken encounters increases, but Shakespeare paces them with masterly skill. He does not mechanically exploit the possibilities inherent in the basic situation, but permits the audience to savour the comedy, as at the beginning of Act II, scene 2, when Antipholus of Syracuse encounters his own Dromio after his meeting with the wrong one. This leads to an episode of incipient seriousness, the first of the play's beatings (line 23), mitigated by the jesting that follows it, which culminates in the first of several static, comic set-pieces, a device by which Shakespeare relaxes the intellectual tension, giving the audience a breathing-space before the next mistaken encounter, between Adriana and the man she takes for her husband. Again the humour of the encounter is not mechanical, because, comic though the situation is, the subject of Adriana's long speech of rebuke is a serious discussion of marriage responsibilities.

It is not until the beginning of Act III that we meet the Ephesian Antipholus, whose appearance helps to give a new impetus to the action, and introduces the plot device of the necklace which he is having made for his wife. Again there is a retrospective discussion of an earlier misunderstanding, followed by a little disputation on the theme of hospitality which has an ironic bearing on what is to follow. This is the most complex misunderstanding so far, in which the Ephesian Antipholus and Dromio are denied entry to their own house. It too is reinforced by a serious speech from Balthasar advocating a patient attempt to assess the situation, which succeeds in averting violence and has the effect of encouraging the Ephesian Antipholus to visit the Courtesan. The following scene, in which Luciana earnestly rebukes her sister's supposed husband and in the process inspires his admiration, is quite un-

Plautine, and creates another serious romantic episode which, though tinged by the comedy of the situation, is more evidence against those who accuse the play of being a mechanical farce. It turns into comedy with the entrance of the Syracusan Dromio in flight from the kitchen wench, but again we have a static set-piece, the brilliantly comic catechism describing Nell. The last episode of the scene returns us to comedy of errors as the merchant, Angelo, delivers to Antipholus of Syracuse the chain ordered by his brother. The comic complications deriving from this are developed in Act IV, scene 1, as a result of which the Ephesian Antipholus is arrested for debt.

Act IV, scene 2, reverts to the retrospective method, deepening the characterization of, especially, Adriana. This scene, too, includes a brief set-piece, on time, just as at the beginning of the following scene there is another, a piece of jesting (obscured for us by the passage of time) between the Syracusan Antipholus and his Dromio. Antipholus's subsequent encounter with the Courtesan, who mistakes him for his brother, parallels his earlier encounter with his brother's wife, though the result here is flight, not the acceptance of offered hospitality. In Act IV, scene 4, confusions result in two beatings for the Ephesian Dromio, who is allowed a lament on his plight (lines 27–37), and also in an attack on the exorcist who comes to try to cure the Ephesian Antipholus of his suspected madness. Another retrospective episode (lines 58–76) results in so intense a confirmation of confusion that the Ephesian master and servant are bound and carried off. The comic climax of the scene comes when their counterparts enter with drawn swords, and frighten the citizens away. But the end of the scene cunningly begins to turn the tide, as the Syracusan Dromio expresses affection for Ephesus and its generous inhabitants.

23

Violence threatens again in the next scene, when the Second Merchant and Antipholus of Syracuse quarrel about the chain; and when the visiting master and slave take refuge in the priory, the impending resolution of the action is signalled by the entry of a new character, the Abbess. Though there is nothing to inform the audience of the fact, Shakespeare is returning now to the material of his framework story.

The Abbess's catechism and rebuke of Adriana, though tinged with comedy, revert to the serious theme of marital responsibilities, and the entry, on his way to execution, of Egeon, who remains silent for some time, is a reminder of the potential seriousness of the action. The recapitulation and re-examination of what has passed force the audience into a full awareness of the situation before the next comic surprise, the account of the violence done by Antipholus and Dromio of Ephesus to Dr Pinch. The scene deepens in seriousness as Antipholus pleads to the Duke for justice, and the bewildered Adriana and Luciana deny the accusations brought against them. Retrospection comes in again in the Ephesian Antipholus's long account of his sufferings, and the scene reaches a high pitch of seriousness in Egeon's lament on being denied by the man he believes to be the son he has brought up.

Appropriately, it is the Abbess who resolves the action when she enters with the Syracusan Antipholus and Dromio. It is a resolution much more complex than that of Plautus's play, for here we have a husband reunited with his wife, two sons with their mother, two sons with their father, twin masters and twin servants with each other, along with the reconciliation of husband and wife, the realization that there is no obstacle to the union of Antipholus of Syracuse with his sister-in-law, the liberation of Egeon from the death penalty, and the clearing up of the business problems. All this is clarified with a mastery of pacing that is deceptive in its ease. Shakespeare's delicacy of touch is nowhere more apparent than in the play's closing lines. Both pairs of twins remain on stage. Confusion is briefly renewed as the Syracusan Dromio addresses the Ephesian Antipholus. But now all is good-humoured. The twin masters leave their servants to rejoice with one another. Again there is a moment of retrospection as the Syracusan Dromio remembers the 'fat friend' who had given him so much trouble, and reflects with relief that she will be no closer than his sister-in-law. Their departure hand in hand makes a lightly cheerful ending after the more strongly emotional reunions that have made it possible.

Though there is no fully developed sub-plot in *The Comedy of Errors*, the exploits of the Dromios mirror, sometimes in distorted fashion, those of their masters. Yet the plot is tightly enough knit for us to feel that Shakespeare does not violate the unity of action. So far as place is concerned, he seems to have been even more anxious to conform to neo-classical practice. The action is set entirely in Ephesus, and is disposed in a manner that appears to imitate the supposed layout of the classical theatre. The play could be acted against a background of three structures, or doors in the rear wall, representing Antipholus's house, with the sign of the Phoenix, in the centre, the Courtesan's house, bearing the sign of the Porpentine, to one side of it, and the priory, with a religious sign, to the other. The main stage could be used for all the action, including the scenes localized in the mart, and the side entrances would be imagined to lead to the bay and to the town. An upper level may have been used (see Commentary to III.1, 'Staging'). This kind of staging seems to be specially related to that commonly used in performances at the Inns of Court, but no doubt it could equally be used in the public theatres.

*

To consider the sources from which Shakespeare derived his plot material, and to examine some of the ways in which he laid it out, is still to leave unexplored the most important aspect of all, that is, the artistic use he made of it, the ways in which it appears to have stimulated his imagination, and the potential significances that he perceived in it. Some of these have necessarily been touched on already, being inextricably involved with the layout of the plot, but I should like to say a little more about them in the following pages.

Menaechmi ends in the selling of a wife. *The Comedy of Errors* is not, like many of Shakespeare's comedies, a play of wooing; but it ends in the re-establishment of two marriages and looks forward to a third. Marital responsibility is a topic towards which Shakespeare's material easily led him, and his attitude to it is much developed from Plautus's easy cynicism. The topic is debated at some length in the first scene involving women characters – Act II, scene 1 – early in which Luciana adjures her sister to be patient. At this stage the word is used merely in relation to time – Adriana's husband is late for lunch. But Adriana argues that women should have equal rights with men, and replies to Luciana's recommendations of obedience with astonishment at her 'Patience unmoved' (line 32). This dialogue establishes divergent values that are to be tested in the course of the play. The episode that follows, in which Adriana threatens Dromio, seems designed to demonstrate her lack of patience. Her sister explicitly rebukes her for it: 'Fie, how impatience loureth in your face' (line 86), and for the 'Self-harming jealousy' to which it leads (lines 102 and 116). Luciana's common sense sets off her sister's aberrations from it.

The jealousy foreshadowed in Act II, scene 1, finds full expression in Adriana's speech in the following scene (II.2.119–55), a speech that would be a serious and moving expression of the anguish of a betrayed wife were it not both unfounded and delivered to the wrong man. The audience is being encouraged to take a somewhat critical attitude towards Adriana, reinforced by her husband's statement 'My wife is shrewish when I keep not hours' (III.1.2). Her behaviour tempts her husband himself to understandable impatience when he finds that he is locked out of his own house, but Balthasar, in his speech beginning 'Have patience, sir', succeeds in reducing him to a reasonable frame of mind, and persuading him to 'Depart in patience' and refrain from jealousy in the hope that Adriana will be able to offer an explanation of what has happened. There is another hint of Adriana's predisposition to jealousy in her husband's statement that she has often, though unjustly, 'upbraided' him with the wench whose society he now goes to seek.

The next stage in the development of the theme is a slightly disconcerting one, when Luciana speaks to her sister's supposed husband and suggests that if he must be unfaithful, he might at least keep quiet about it (III.2.7–28; for a possible explanation of this, see the Commentary). In Act IV, scene 2, Adriana questions Luciana about her supposed husband's wooing of her sister, and again has to be implored to 'Have patience' (line 16). In a potentially touching passage she reacts with a vituperative attack on her husband which she immediately retracts, admitting 'I think him better than I say' (line 25); and at the end of the scene she hands over to Dromio the money that her husband needs.

The climax comes in the last scene, when Adriana pleads with the Abbess to release the man she believes to be her husband. He is mad, she says. Perhaps his melancholy was the result of illicit love, says the Abbess. Adriana agrees that this is possible. The Abbess suggests that she ought to have reprehended him. Adriana replies that she did. And step by step the Abbess leads Adriana into an admission that she has used 'The venom clamours of a jealous woman' (V.1.69), and that it is her 'jealous fits' that have 'scared thy husband from the use of wits'. Adriana, in spite of her sister's efforts to defend her, admits the justice of the accusations. It is a neat piece of stagecraft, most clearly paralleled in Shakespeare's later work by the way in which the Duke in *Measure for Measure* forces Isabella into a position where she can only plead for mercy on behalf of Angelo. After this, Adriana agrees to behave towards her husband with a full sense of her duty – rather as Luciana had recommended (II.1.15–25); but still the Abbess has to require her to 'Be patient' (V.1.102). Adriana's relationship with her husband, then, is made the basis for a sequence of corrective comedy, in which the wife is brought to an understanding of flaws in her relationship with her husband.

Shakespeare's awareness of the relevance to his story of ideas about marriage may have been stimulated by the fact that the wife in the tale from which he derived his framework narrative takes refuge in the temple of Diana at Ephesus. This could easily have recalled to him St Paul's visit to Ephesus, recounted in Acts 19, and his Epistle to the Ephesians. It was difficult for an Elizabethan not to be familiar with the Bible, and it is quite likely that St Paul's remarks on the duty of a wife to submit herself to her husband, on the reciprocal duty of a husband to love his wife, and on the relationships between masters and servants, coloured the play. (The most important parallels are recorded in the Commentary to this edition.)

A broader topic than the relationship between husband and wife, though clearly related to it, is that of family relationships in general. Shakespeare draws our attention to the link by a subtle use of recurrent poetic images which foreshadows the complex developments of this technique in his later plays. The first scene has told us of a family that has been dispersed. Since the agent of separation was the sea it is appropriate that Antipholus, seeking his brother, should liken himself to a drop of water in the ocean:

> *I to the world am like a drop of water*
> *That in the ocean seeks another drop,*
> *Who, falling there to find his fellow forth,*
> *Unseen, inquisitive, confounds himself.*
> *So I, to find a mother and a brother,*
> *In quest of them unhappy, lose myself.* I.2.35–40

The image is powerful not only as a representation of what has already happened, but also by anticipation, because Antipholus is shortly to 'lose' himself in a way that he cannot foresee. He will not merely give up his own concerns while seeking his brother, but will also, by being treated as if he were someone other than he really is, be made to feel that he has lost his own identity (II.2.205).

Adriana picks up the same image when she describes the relationship between herself and her husband:

> *How comes it now, my husband, O how comes it,*
> *That thou art then estrangèd from thyself?*
> *Thyself I call it, being strange to me*
> *That, undividable, incorporate,*
> *Am better than thy dear self's better part.*

> *Ah, do not tear away thyself from me;*
> *For know, my love, as easy mayst thou fall*
> *A drop of water in the breaking gulf,*
> *And take unmingled thence that drop again*
> *Without addition or diminishing,*
> *As take from me thyself, and not me too.*
>
> II.2.128–38

The breaking of the relationship is seen as something that must be harmful to both parties. Sea-imagery is used again to convey the idea of the merging of personalities in a love-relationship in the lines in which Antipholus declares his passion for Luciana:

> *O, train me not, sweet mermaid, with thy note*
> *To drown me in thy sister's flood of tears.*
> *Sing, siren, for thyself, and I will dote.*
> *Spread o'er the silver waves thy golden hairs*
> *And as a bed I'll take thee, and there lie,*
> *And in that glorious supposition think*
> *He gains by death that hath such means to die.*
> *Let love, being light, be drownèd if she sink.*
>
> III.2.45–52

All these passages stress the idea of loss of personality, whether painfully, by the separation from or bereavement of loved ones, or fruitfully, through a giving in union which is also a transformation. Antipholus of Syracuse's vision of happiness with Luciana looks forward to the end of the play, when this vision or 'dream' (V.1.377) becomes something that he can hope 'to make good', and when all the main characters gain a new confidence in their identity – almost a sense of rebirth (see V.1.401–7) – as a result of the rectifying of the errors.

The idea that separation diminishes the personality is

relevant to the comic confusions of the action, which are consequent on the presence of two pairs of twins. Of course, twins are rarely exactly alike. It is sometimes suggested that Shakespeare's use of twins was impractical since a theatre company can rarely contain actors who resemble one another enough to represent them satisfactorily, but this, it seems to me, is fallacious. A director who could call on the services of identical twins for this play would probably be wise not to do so. Though it is useful that the actors should be like enough for it not to seem too implausible that they should be mistaken for one another, it is most important that the audience should always know which is which. The concept of the absolute external identity of one person with another is easily productive of comedy; but it is also frightening. It is a concept that Shakespeare, as the father of twins, had special reason to ponder. It brings home to us the mysteries of the human personality, the fact that our sense of identity does not only come from within but depends too upon a high degree of constancy in the reactions of those around us. If we suddenly found ourselves not recognized by our family, madness could well result. In *King Lear*, Shakespeare profoundly explores the effect on the King of such a reversal of expected behaviour from his family and subjects. And in *The Comedy of Errors* he exploits more than the simply comic possibilities of the notion.

Besides having connexions with St Paul, Ephesus was also biblically associated with witchcraft and magic, and this may have influenced Shakespeare in another important sequence of ideas that enrich the action. It is a sequence that, starting from the feeling of strangeness induced by the errors of the plot, extends in a variety of ways including the possibilities that the odd happenings are the result of aberrations within the characters – that they are dreaming, or mad – or of some evil practice upon them, resulting in a deprivation or metamorphosis of identity. One reason why this is dramatically useful is simply that it diverts our attention from the failure of central characters to deduce the true cause of the errors. Thus, Antipholus of Syracuse, addressed at length by Adriana under the illusion that he is her husband, wonders if he was married to her in a dream, or if he dreams now (II.2.191–2, 223), but his Dromio attributes their plight rather to supernatural agency: 'We talk with goblins, owls, and sprites' (line 199), and fears that he has been 'transformed' to an ape. His master counters that he is more like an ass, and early in the following scene the other Antipholus similarly accuses his Dromio. Antipholus of Syracuse suggests, and indeed begs for, a different kind of transformation under a beneficent supernatural influence when, falling in love with Luciana, he asks:

> Are you a god? Would you create me new?
> Transform me, then, and to your power I'll yield.
>
> III.2.39–40

She suspects that he is mad (line 53). His Dromio's account of how he was wooed by the kitchen wench begins with him questioning his own identity (III.2.73–4) and culminates in a passage that sustains the sequence of ideas – she seemed to know him so well, though he had never seen her before, that he 'ran from her as a witch' and felt that he had been in danger of being 'transformed' into a dog (lines 152–4).

Antipholus sounds the theme strongly after the play's initial error, his first encounter with the wrong Dromio:

> They say this town is full of cozenage,
> As nimble jugglers that deceive the eye,
> Dark-working sorcerers that change the mind,

Soul-killing witches that deform the body,
Disguisèd cheaters, prating mountebanks,
And many suchlike liberties of sin. I.2.97–102

Not surprisingly, then, he suspects supernatural influence when he finds that he is treated as an old acquaintance by the inhabitants of Ephesus, fearing that 'Lapland sorcerers inhabit here' (IV.3.11), that both he and his servant are 'distract' and 'wander in illusions' (lines 42–3), and that the Courtesan is the devil (lines 50 and 79). His behaviour causes the Courtesan to suspect him of madness, a theme which reaches a climax in Act IV, scene 4, when Dr Pinch is brought in to cure him. Pinch is another character who is easily burlesqued. His role is tiny. He appears in only one scene, and speaks only twelve lines. Yet he is a scene-stealing figure. As a new character appearing at a climax of confusion, he makes a strong impact. His function as an exorcist serves as a justification for the invention of elaborate comic business as he confronts Antipholus (of Ephesus). The confrontation is exceptionally violent. And the brilliant description of him and his actions later in the play (V.1.237–54) justifies the presentation of him as grotesque in appearance.

It is the suspicion that Antipholus and Dromio of Syracuse (mistaken for their counterparts of Ephesus) are mad that precipitates the resolution of the action, as they take refuge in the priory and come under the care of the Abbess, Antipholus's mother. The notion of transformation reaches its climax when the Duke, bewildered by the contradictory accounts offered to him, declares 'I think you all have drunk of Circe's cup' (V.1.271). A little later he says he thinks they are all 'mated, or stark mad' (line 282); and, seeing the twins together, he declares that one of them must be '*genius*' – attendant spirit – to the other.

Egeon, confronting his long-lost wife, thinks he may be dreaming (line 353), and Antipholus of Syracuse fears the same as he renews his suit to Luciana (line 377). The figure who reveals the order beneath the apparent chaos is that eminently sane lady, the Abbess Æmilia, Egeon's wife. She is strong enough to show Adriana the error of her ways (not all the 'errors' of the title are the result of external confusion), but she is also, appropriately, an explicitly Christian figure. On her first appearance we hear that in treating Antipholus's supposed madness she will use, not the brutal methods of Dr Pinch, but 'wholesome syrups, drugs, and holy prayers'. Under her influence her husband, sentenced to die under a retaliatory law, is freed. She provides information about the past which helps to explain the mystery. It is interesting that at the end of the play she seems to displace the Duke. In the first scene he had been a representative of justice, though not an unsympathetic one: 'we may pity, though not pardon thee' (I.1.98). In the last scene, under the Abbess's influence, he becomes merciful, too, refusing the ducats offered by Antipholus of Ephesus for his father's ransom. The speech that rounds off the main action is made by the Abbess, and the Duke contentedly agrees to be one of the company at the feast that will symbolize the final re-establishment of order and harmony.

The fundamental human emotions on which *The Comedy of Errors* can base its claim to be comedy rather than farce are the simple and related ones of sorrow at separation and joy in reunion, and the figure on whom they are most intensely concentrated is Egeon. It is essential that, in any performance of the play not intended as a travesty, Egeon should be played sympathetically. We first see him in despair, having failed in his search for his family and now condemned to die unless within a few hours he can find someone to redeem him. This establishes very solidly a framework of time within which the action will unfold. His execution is threatened for sunset (I.1.28 and I.2.7). During the body of the play we are not explicitly reminded of his impending fate, but we can scarcely forget him altogether as we follow his sons' adventures. And we are often made aware of the passage of time towards the hour appointed for his death. (See Commentary to I.2.26.)

The strong and rather melancholy sense of the natural flow of time created by the opening scene is immediately shattered in the first of the play's mistaken encounters. Dromio has not 'returned so soon' but 'Rather approached too late' (I.2.42–3); and from this point onwards confusion about time is one of the comic consequences of mistaken identity. 'The action', as Gāmini Salgādo writes, 'takes the form of a series of broken appointments, circumscribed by one appointment that is scrupulously kept (the Duke's meeting at five o'clock with Egeon).' The idea is brought to the surface in the comic set-piece on time between Antipholus and Dromio of Syracuse (II.2.70–118), which has something of the tone later to be heard in music-hall 'routines', and is lightly concerned with the notion that 'There's a time for all things'.

It might almost be suggested that *The Comedy of Errors* is a kind of pastoral play in which an apparent freeing of the characters from the normal processes of time takes the place of the liberation from the restrictions of ordered society which Shakespeare adumbrates in *The Two Gentlemen of Verona* and develops more fully in such varied plays as *A Midsummer Night's Dream*, *As You Like It*, *King Lear*, and *The Tempest*. In those plays, characters gain in maturity as a result of their temporary displacement, finally displaying a heightened sense of responsibility which enables them to realize themselves more fully within the bounds of society. So in *The Comedy of Errors*, when the confusions involving time are resolved, the characters find a new stability in their relationships. This resolution approaches at the moment of highest complication. All the normal relationships of the main figures of the play have been cast into disorder when Egeon enters in solemn procession to

> *the melancholy vale,*
> *The place of death and sorry execution*
> *Behind the ditches of the abbey here.*
>
> V.i.120–22

His emotion on being rejected by the man whom he believes to be the son he has tended from birth, and by Dromio, is given full expression:

> *O, grief hath changed me since you saw me last,*
> *And careful hours with time's deformèd hand*
> *Have written strange defeatures in my face.*
>
> V.i.298–300

They do not even recognize his voice:

> *Not know my voice? O time's extremity,*
> *Hast thou so cracked and splitted my poor tongue*
> *In seven short years that here my only son*
> *Knows not my feeble key of untuned cares?*
> *Though now this grainèd face of mine be hid*
> *In sap-consuming winter's drizzled snow,*
> *And all the conduits of my blood froze up,*
> *Yet hath my night of life some memory,*
> *My wasting lamps some fading glimmer left,*
> *My dull deaf ears a little use to hear.*
> *All these old witnesses, I cannot err,*
> *Tell me thou art my son Antipholus.*
>
> V.i.308–19

This episode is climactically placed as the strongest emotional point of the play. And it is interesting that Egeon bemoaning his apparent rejection by his son is very close in sentiment to the terms in which Adriana had mourned the apparent loss of her husband. She too was moved to question her own identity, to wonder whether she was much changed from what she had been:

> Hath homely age the alluring beauty took
> From my poor cheek? Then he hath wasted it.
> Are my discourses dull? barren my wit? . . .
> What ruins are in me that can be found
> By him not ruined? Then is he the ground
> Of my defeatures. My decayèd fair
> A sunny look of his would soon repair.

II.1.89–91, 96–9

The fact that the central characters have been sympathetically presented throughout the play, that we have been aware of their anxieties, their capacity to suffer and to feel humiliation –

> perhaps, my son,
> Thou shamest to acknowledge me in misery

says Egeon (V.1.322–3) – helps us to feel the happiness of the play's resolution. It is not written very fully into the speeches, but it is surely there, behind the thought of Egeon that he may be dreaming, behind the good-humoured participation of the Duke in the multiple recognitions, behind Antipholus of Syracuse's renewed suit to Luciana, behind the satisfactory resolution of the business dealings and the Courtesan's retrieval of her ring. As so often in his comedies, and with great theatrical tact, Shakespeare sets the full expression of happiness forward to a point beyond the end of the action, the feast at which all will be explained, and all who have suffered wrong will be rewarded. The play ends with images of birth and rebirth, on a serious level in the Abbess's final lines:

> *Thirty-three years have I but gone in travail*
> *Of you, my sons, and till this present hour*
> *My heavy burden ne'er deliverèd.*
> *The Duke, my husband, and my children both,*
> *And you, the calendars of their nativity,*
> *Go to a gossips' feast, and go with me.*
> *After so long grief, such nativity*

and more lightly from Dromio in his final couplet:

> *We came into the world like brother and brother,*
> *And now let's go hand in hand, not one before another.*

Reunited, the twin servants are defined by one another – 'I see by you I am a sweet-faced youth'. Each has his own identity, yet is related harmoniously to the other. And, after all, the play ends, like Plautus's, with a verbal and visual emphasis on brotherly love as they join hands in a gesture of honest affection that epitomizes the characteristically Shakespearian fusion of gaiety with seriousness here achieved for, probably, the first time.

FURTHER READING

Texts

The fullest edition of *The Comedy of Errors* is by R. A. Foakes
in the new Arden series (1962). The present edition is much
indebted to it. It has an excellent introduction and valuable
notes. John Dover Wilson's edition in the New Cambridge
Shakespeare (1922, revised 1962), with an introduction by
Arthur Quiller-Couch, is by now badly dated. The Signet
edition (New York, 1965), prepared by Harry Levin, has a
good critical introduction and reprints Warner's translation of
Menaechmi.

The original text of the play is best read in *The Norton
Facsimile of the First Folio of Shakespeare*, prepared by Charlton
Hinman (New York, 1968). Textual work on the play is usefully
summarized in R. A. Foakes's edition. Important earlier studies
are those in E. K. Chambers's *William Shakespeare: A Study
of Facts and Problems* (2 volumes, Oxford, 1930), I, 305–12, and
in W. W. Greg's *The Shakespeare First Folio* (Oxford, 1955).
Specific textual points are discussed in C. J. Sisson's *New
Readings in Shakespeare* (2 volumes, 1956) and S. A. Tannen-
baum's 'Notes on *The Comedy of Errors*', *Shakespeare Jahrbuch*
68 (1932), 103–24.

Sources, Date, and Background

There is a valuable essay on the play's sources in Geoffrey
Bullough's *Narrative and Dramatic Sources of Shakespeare*,
Volume I (1957), which also reprints Warner's translation of
Menaechmi and extracts from Plautus's *Amphitruo* and Gower's
Confessio Amantis. Plautus's original play is edited with a
translation by Paul Nixon in the Loeb Classical Library,
Plautus, Volume II (1917). The play's background in romance

literature is surveyed in Stanley Wells's 'Shakespeare and Romance' (*Later Shakespeare*, Stratford-upon-Avon Studies 8 (1966), pages 49–79, reprinted in *Shakespeare's Later Comedies*, edited by D. J. Palmer (Penguin Shakespeare Library, 1971), pages 117–42, where, however, the section specifically on *The Comedy of Errors* is omitted), and in Carol Gesner's *Shakespeare and the Greek Romance* (Lexington, Kentucky, 1971). The date of the play has been much discussed; again, R. A. Foakes's Introduction should be consulted. Sidney Thomas's article 'The Date of *The Comedy of Errors*', *Shakespeare Quarterly* 7 (1956), 377–84, arguing for 1594, is worth consideration, though inconclusive. T. W. Baldwin's *On the Compositional Genetics of 'The Comedy of Errors'* (Urbana, Illinois, 1965) is a massive study useful only to the specialist. *Gesta Grayorum* (see Introduction, page 10) is available in a Malone Society Reprint (1914) and in an edition by Desmond Bland (Liverpool, 1968). The play's stage history is usefully surveyed in R. A. Foakes's edition.

Criticism

E. K. Chambers has a concise and sensible essay in *Shakespeare: A Survey* (1925; Penguin Books, 1964). G. R. Elliott published a suggestive essay called 'Weirdness in *The Comedy of Errors*', *University of Toronto Quarterly* 55 (1939), 95–106, reprinted in *Shakespeare's Comedies*, edited by Laurence Lerner (Penguin Shakespeare Library, 1967). H. B. Charlton's chapter in his *Shakespearean Comedy* (1938) is mostly concerned with the play's connexions with Roman comedy. In *Shakespeare and His Comedies* (1957; revised 1962), John Russell Brown writes on the play's concerns with love, and finds that it deals 'not with the joys of giving in love, but with the follies and evils of possessiveness'. Bertrand Evans, in *Shakespeare's Comedies* (Oxford, 1960), writes on Shakespeare's dramatic technique in the play. Probably the best single study is Harold Brooks's 'Themes and Structure in *The Comedy of Errors*' (*Early Shakespeare*, Stratford-upon-Avon Studies 3 (1961), pages 55–71), which includes some perceptive and detailed structural analysis.

R. A. Foakes's Introduction includes a valuable critical account of the play, with wide reference to earlier criticism. E. M. W. Tillyard, in *Shakespeare's Early Comedies* (1966), shows a keen appreciation especially of Shakespeare's intellectual achievement in the play: 'There is indeed something massive about the intellectual power Shakespeare here displays: a power of holding in suspense in the mind a vast quantity of detail and of being able to call on any item in it at the shortest notice.' Gāmini Salgādo's '"Time's Deformèd Hand": Sequence, Consequence, and Inconsequence in *The Comedy of Errors*' (*Shakespeare Survey 25*, 1972) is an illuminating study of the play's concern with time.

THE COMEDY OF ERRORS

THE CHARACTERS IN THE PLAY

Solinus, DUKE of Ephesus
EGEON, a merchant of Syracuse
Æmilia, Lady ABBESS at Ephesus, and Egeon's wife
ANTIPHOLUS OF EPHESUS ⎱ twin brothers, sons of
ANTIPHOLUS OF SYRACUSE ⎰ Egeon and Æmilia
DROMIO OF EPHESUS ⎱ twin brothers, bondsmen to
DROMIO OF SYRACUSE ⎰ the Antipholus twins
ADRIANA, wife of Antipholus of Ephesus
LUCIANA, her sister
LUCE (also referred to as Nell), Adriana's kitchen-maid
BALTHASAR, a merchant
ANGELO, a goldsmith
Doctor PINCH, a schoolmaster
FIRST MERCHANT
SECOND MERCHANT
An OFFICER
A COURTESAN
A MESSENGER

Gaoler, Officers, Headsman, and other attendants

Enter Solinus, Duke of Ephesus, with Egeon, the
merchant of Syracuse, Gaoler, and other attendants

EGEON

    Proceed, Solinus, to procure my fall,
    And by the doom of death end woes and all.

DUKE

    Merchant of Syracusa, plead no more.
    I am not partial to infringe our laws.
    The enmity and discord which of late
    Sprung from the rancorous outrage of your Duke
    To merchants, our well-dealing countrymen,
    Who, wanting guilders to redeem their lives,
    Have sealed his rigorous statutes with their bloods,
    Excludes all pity from our threatening looks.   10
    For since the mortal and intestine jars
    'Twixt thy seditious countrymen and us
    It hath in solemn synods been decreed
    Both by the Syracusians and ourselves
    To admit no traffic to our adverse towns.
    Nay, more:
    If any born at Ephesus be seen
    At any Syracusian marts and fairs;
    Again, if any Syracusian born
    Come to the bay of Ephesus, he dies,   20
    His goods confiscate to the Duke's dispose,
    Unless a thousand marks be levièd
    To quit the penalty and to ransom him.
    Thy substance, valued at the highest rate,

Cannot amount unto a hundred marks;
Therefore by law thou art condemned to die.

EGEON

Yet this my comfort: when your words are done,
My woes end likewise with the evening sun.

DUKE

Well, Syracusian, say in brief the cause
30 Why thou departed'st from thy native home,
And for what cause thou camest to Ephesus.

EGEON

A heavier task could not have been imposed
Than I to speak my griefs unspeakable.
Yet, that the world may witness that my end
Was wrought by nature, not by vile offence,
I'll utter what my sorrow gives me leave.
In Syracusa was I born, and wed
Unto a woman happy but for me,
And by me, had not our hap been bad.
40 With her I lived in joy, our wealth increased
By prosperous voyages I often made
To Epidamnum, till my factor's death,
And the great care of goods at random left,
Drew me from kind embracements of my spouse,
From whom my absence was not six months old
Before herself, almost at fainting under
The pleasing punishment that women bear,
Had made provision for her following me,
And soon and safe arrivèd where I was.
50 There had she not been long but she became
A joyful mother of two goodly sons;
And, which was strange, the one so like the other
As could not be distinguished but by names.
That very hour, and in the self-same inn,
A mean woman was deliverèd

Of such a burden male, twins both alike.
Those, for their parents were exceeding poor,
I bought, and brought up to attend my sons.
My wife, not meanly proud of two such boys,
Made daily motions for our home return.   60
Unwilling I agreed. Alas, too soon
We came aboard.
A league from Epidamnum had we sailed
Before the always wind-obeying deep
Gave any tragic instance of our harm.
But longer did we not retain much hope,
For what obscurèd light the heavens did grant
Did but convey unto our fearful minds
A doubtful warrant of immediate death,
Which though myself would gladly have embraced,   70
Yet the incessant weepings of my wife,
Weeping before for what she saw must come,
And piteous plainings of the pretty babes,
That mourned for fashion, ignorant what to fear,
Forced me to seek delays for them and me.
And this it was – for other means was none –
The sailors sought for safety by our boat,
And left the ship, then sinking-ripe, to us.
My wife, more careful for the latter-born,
Had fastened him unto a small spare mast   80
Such as seafaring men provide for storms.
To him one of the other twins was bound,
Whilst I had been like heedful of the other.
The children thus disposed, my wife and I,
Fixing our eyes on whom our care was fixed,
Fastened ourselves at either end the mast,
And floating straight, obedient to the stream,
Was carried towards Corinth, as we thought.
At length the sun, gazing upon the earth,

90   Dispersed those vapours that offended us,
And by the benefit of his wished light
The seas waxed calm, and we discoverèd
Two ships from far, making amain to us:
Of Corinth that, of Epidaurus this.
But ere they came – O, let me say no more.
Gather the sequel by that went before!

DUKE

Nay, forward, old man; do not break off so,
For we may pity, though not pardon thee.

EGEON

O, had the gods done so, I had not now
100   Worthily termed them merciless to us;
For ere the ships could meet by twice five leagues
We were encountered by a mighty rock,
Which being violently borne upon,
Our helpful ship was splitted in the midst;
So that in this unjust divorce of us
Fortune had left to both of us alike
What to delight in, what to sorrow for.
Her part, poor soul, seeming as burdenèd
With lesser weight but not with lesser woe,
110   Was carried with more speed before the wind,
And in our sight they three were taken up
By fishermen of Corinth, as we thought.
At length another ship had seized on us,
And knowing whom it was their hap to save
Gave healthful welcome to their shipwrecked guests,
And would have reft the fishers of their prey
Had not their bark been very slow of sail;
And therefore homeward did they bend their course.
Thus have you heard me severed from my bliss,
120   That by misfortunes was my life prolonged
To tell sad stories of my own mishaps.

DUKE

And for the sake of them thou sorrowest for,
Do me the favour to dilate at full
What have befallen of them and thee till now.

EGEON

My youngest boy, and yet my eldest care,
At eighteen years became inquisitive
After his brother, and importuned me
That his attendant, so his case was like,
Reft of his brother, but retained his name,
Might bear him company in the quest of him;   130
Whom whilst I laboured of a love to see,
I hazarded the loss of whom I loved.
Five summers have I spent in farthest Greece,
Roaming clean through the bounds of Asia,
And coasting homeward came to Ephesus,
Hopeless to find, yet loath to leave unsought
Or that or any place that harbours men.
But here must end the story of my life,
And happy were I in my timely death
Could all my travels warrant me they live.   140

DUKE

Hapless Egeon, whom the fates have marked
To bear the extremity of dire mishap,
Now trust me, were it not against our laws,
Against my crown, my oath, my dignity,
Which princes, would they, may not disannul,
My soul should sue as advocate for thee.
But though thou art adjudgèd to the death,
And passèd sentence may not be recalled
But to our honour's great disparagement,
Yet will I favour thee in what I can.   150
Therefore, merchant, I'll limit thee this day
To seek thy health by beneficial help.

Try all the friends thou hast in Ephesus;
Beg thou or borrow to make up the sum,
And live. If no, then thou art doomed to die.
Gaoler, take him to thy custody.

GAOLER

I will, my lord.

EGEON

Hopeless and helpless doth Egeon wend,
But to procrastinate his lifeless end.   *Exeunt*

I.2   *Enter Antipholus of Syracuse, First Merchant, and*
            Dromio of Syracuse

FIRST MERCHANT

Therefore give out you are of Epidamnum
Lest that your goods too soon be confiscate.
This very day a Syracusian merchant
Is apprehended for arrival here,
And, not being able to buy out his life,
According to the statute of the town
Dies ere the weary sun set in the west.
There is your money that I had to keep.

ANTIPHOLUS OF SYRACUSE (*to Dromio of Syracuse*)

Go, bear it to the Centaur, where we host,

10   And stay there, Dromio, till I come to thee.
Within this hour it will be dinner-time.
Till that I'll view the manners of the town,
Peruse the traders, gaze upon the buildings,
And then return and sleep within mine inn;
For with long travel I am stiff and weary.
Get thee away.

DROMIO OF SYRACUSE

Many a man would take you at your word
And go indeed, having so good a mean.   *Exit*

ANTIPHOLUS OF SYRACUSE
  A trusty villain, sir, that very oft,
  When I am dull with care and melancholy,   20
  Lightens my humour with his merry jests.
  What, will you walk with me about the town,
  And then go to my inn and dine with me?

FIRST MERCHANT
  I am invited, sir, to certain merchants,
  Of whom I hope to make much benefit.
  I crave your pardon. Soon at five o'clock,
  Please you, I'll meet with you upon the mart,
  And afterward consort you till bedtime.
  My present business calls me from you now.

ANTIPHOLUS OF SYRACUSE
  Farewell till then. I will go lose myself   30
  And wander up and down to view the city.

FIRST MERCHANT
  Sir, I commend you to your own content.   *Exit*

ANTIPHOLUS OF SYRACUSE
  He that commends me to mine own content
  Commends me to the thing I cannot get.
  I to the world am like a drop of water
  That in the ocean seeks another drop,
  Who, falling there to find his fellow forth,
  Unseen, inquisitive, confounds himself.
  So I, to find a mother and a brother,
  In quest of them unhappy, lose myself.   40
    Enter Dromio of Ephesus
  Here comes the almanac of my true date.
  What now? How chance thou art returned so soon?

DROMIO OF EPHESUS
  Returned so soon? Rather approached too late.
  The capon burns, the pig falls from the spit.
  The clock hath strucken twelve upon the bell;

My mistress made it one upon my cheek.
She is so hot because the meat is cold.
The meat is cold because you come not home.
You come not home because you have no stomach.
50   You have no stomach, having broke your fast.
But we that know what 'tis to fast and pray
Are penitent for your default today.

ANTIPHOLUS OF SYRACUSE

Stop in your wind, sir. Tell me this, I pray:
Where have you left the money that I gave you?

DROMIO OF EPHESUS

O, sixpence that I had o' Wednesday last
To pay the saddler for my mistress' crupper.
The saddler had it, sir. I kept it not.

ANTIPHOLUS OF SYRACUSE

I am not in a sportive humour now.
Tell me, and dally not: where is the money?
60   We being strangers here, how darest thou trust
So great a charge from thine own custody?

DROMIO OF EPHESUS

I pray you, jest, sir, as you sit at dinner.
I from my mistress come to you in post.
If I return I shall be post indeed,
For she will scour your fault upon my pate.
Methinks your maw, like mine, should be your clock
And strike you home without a messenger.

ANTIPHOLUS OF SYRACUSE

Come, Dromio, come, these jests are out of season.
Reserve them till a merrier hour than this.
70   Where is the gold I gave in charge to thee?

DROMIO OF EPHESUS

To me, sir? Why, you gave no gold to me!

ANTIPHOLUS OF SYRACUSE

Come on, sir knave, have done your foolishness,

And tell me how thou hast disposed thy charge.

DROMIO OF EPHESUS

My charge was but to fetch you from the mart
Home to your house, the Phoenix, sir, to dinner.
My mistress and her sister stays for you.

ANTIPHOLUS OF SYRACUSE

Now, as I am a Christian, answer me
In what safe place you have bestowed my money,
Or I shall break that merry sconce of yours
That stands on tricks when I am undisposed.   80
Where is the thousand marks thou hadst of me?

DROMIO OF EPHESUS

I have some marks of yours upon my pate,
Some of my mistress' marks upon my shoulders,
But not a thousand marks between you both.
If I should pay your worship those again,
Perchance you will not bear them patiently.

ANTIPHOLUS OF SYRACUSE

Thy mistress' marks? What mistress, slave, hast thou?

DROMIO OF EPHESUS

Your worship's wife, my mistress at the Phoenix;
She that doth fast till you come home to dinner,
And prays that you will hie you home to dinner.   90

ANTIPHOLUS OF SYRACUSE

What, wilt thou flout me thus unto my face,
Being forbid? There, take you that, sir knave.
    He beats Dromio

DROMIO OF EPHESUS

What mean you, sir? For God's sake hold your hands.
Nay, an you will not, sir, I'll take my heels.   *Exit*

ANTIPHOLUS OF SYRACUSE

Upon my life, by some device or other
The villain is o'er-raught of all my money.
They say this town is full of cozenage,

As nimble jugglers that deceive the eye,
Dark-working sorcerers that change the mind,
100 Soul-killing witches that deform the body,
Disguisèd cheaters, prating mountebanks,
And many suchlike liberties of sin.
If it prove so, I will be gone the sooner.
I'll to the Centaur to go seek this slave.
I greatly fear my money is not safe.   *Exit*

*

II.1   *Enter Adriana, wife of Antipholus of Ephesus, with*
              Luciana, her sister

ADRIANA
Neither my husband nor the slave returned,
That in such haste I sent to seek his master?
Sure, Luciana, it is two o'clock.

LUCIANA
Perhaps some merchant hath invited him,
And from the mart he's somewhere gone to dinner.
Good sister, let us dine, and never fret.
A man is master of his liberty.
Time is their master, and when they see time
They'll go or come. If so, be patient, sister.

ADRIANA
10 Why should their liberty than ours be more?

LUCIANA
Because their business still lies out o'door.

ADRIANA
Look when I serve him so he takes it ill.

LUCIANA
O, know he is the bridle of your will.

ADRIANA
There's none but asses will be bridled so.

56

LUCIANA

> Why, headstrong liberty is lashed with woe.
> There's nothing situate under heaven's eye
> But hath his bound in earth, in sea, in sky.
> The beasts, the fishes, and the wingèd fowls
> Are their males' subjects, and at their controls.
> Man, more divine, the master of all these,   20
> Lord of the wide world and wild watery seas,
> Indued with intellectual sense and souls,
> Of more pre-eminence than fish and fowls,
> Are masters to their females, and their lords.
> Then let your will attend on their accords.

ADRIANA

> This servitude makes you to keep unwed.

LUCIANA

> Not this, but troubles of the marriage-bed.

ADRIANA

> But were you wedded, you would bear some sway.

LUCIANA

> Ere I learn love, I'll practise to obey.

ADRIANA

> How if your husband start some otherwhere?   30

LUCIANA

> Till he come home again I would forbear.

ADRIANA

> Patience unmoved! No marvel though she pause.
> They can be meek that have no other cause.
> A wretched soul, bruised with adversity,
> We bid be quiet when we hear it cry.
> But were we burdened with like weight of pain,
> As much or more we should ourselves complain.
> So thou, that hast no unkind mate to grieve thee,
> With urging helpless patience would relieve me.
> But if thou live to see like right bereft,   40

57

This fool-begged patience in thee will be left.

LUCIANA

Well, I will marry one day, but to try.

Here comes your man. Now is your husband nigh.

Enter Dromio of Ephesus

ADRIANA

Say, is your tardy master now at hand?

DROMIO OF EPHESUS Nay, he's at two hands with me, and that my two ears can witness.

ADRIANA

Say, didst thou speak with him? Knowest thou his mind?

DROMIO OF EPHESUS

I? Ay. He told his mind upon mine ear.

Beshrew his hand, I scarce could understand it.

50 LUCIANA Spake he so doubtfully thou couldst not feel his meaning?

DROMIO OF EPHESUS Nay, he struck so plainly I could too well feel his blows, and withal so doubtfully that I could scarce understand them.

ADRIANA

But say, I prithee, is he coming home?

It seems he hath great care to please his wife.

DROMIO OF EPHESUS

Why, mistress, sure my master is horn-mad.

ADRIANA

Horn-mad, thou villain?

DROMIO OF EPHESUS   I mean not cuckold-mad,

But sure he is stark mad.

60 When I desired him to come home to dinner

He asked me for a thousand marks in gold.

' 'Tis dinner-time,' quoth I. 'My gold,' quoth he.

'Your meat doth burn,' quoth I. 'My gold,' quoth he.

'Will you come?' quoth I. 'My gold,' quoth he.

'Where is the thousand marks I gave thee, villain?'
'The pig', quoth I, 'is burned.' 'My gold,' quoth he.
'My mistress, sir –' quoth I – 'Hang up thy mistress!
I know not thy mistress. Out on thy mistress!'

LUCIANA
Quoth who?

DROMIO OF EPHESUS
Quoth my master. 70
'I know', quoth he, 'no house, no wife, no mistress.'
So that my errand, due unto my tongue,
I thank him, I bare home upon my shoulders;
For, in conclusion, he did beat me there.

ADRIANA
Go back again, thou slave, and fetch him home.

DROMIO OF EPHESUS
Go back again and be new-beaten home?
For God's sake send some other messenger.

ADRIANA
Back, slave, or I will break thy pate across.

DROMIO OF EPHESUS
An he will bless that cross with other beating,
Between you I shall have a holy head. 80

ADRIANA
Hence, prating peasant, fetch thy master home.
        She beats Dromio

DROMIO OF EPHESUS
Am I so round with you as you with me
That like a football you do spurn me thus?
You spurn me hence, and he will spurn me hither.
If I last in this service you must case me in leather. *Exit*

LUCIANA (*to Adriana*)
Fie, how impatience loureth in your face.

ADRIANA
His company must do his minions grace

59

Whilst I at home starve for a merry look.
Hath homely age the alluring beauty took
90　From my poor cheek? Then he hath wasted it.
Are my discourses dull? barren my wit?
If voluble and sharp discourse be marred,
Unkindness blunts it more than marble hard.
Do their gay vestments his affections bait?
That's not my fault; he's master of my state.
What ruins are in me that can be found
By him not ruined? Then is he the ground
Of my defeatures. My decayèd fair
A sunny look of his would soon repair.
100　But, too unruly deer, he breaks the pale
And feeds from home. Poor I am but his stale.

LUCIANA
Self-harming jealousy! Fie, beat it hence.

ADRIANA
Unfeeling fools can with such wrongs dispense.
I know his eye doth homage otherwhere,
Or else what lets it but he would be here?
Sister, you know he promised me a chain.
Would that alone a love he would detain
So he would keep fair quarter with his bed.
I see the jewel best enamellèd
110　Will lose his beauty. Yet the gold bides still
That others touch; and often touching will
Wear gold, and no man that hath a name
But falsehood and corruption doth it shame.
Since that my beauty cannot please his eye,
I'll weep what's left away, and weeping die.

LUCIANA
How many fond fools serve mad jealousy!　　*Exeunt*

ANTIPHOLUS OF SYRACUSE

The gold I gave to Dromio is laid up
Safe at the Centaur, and the heedful slave
Is wandered forth in care to seek me out
By computation and mine host's report.
I could not speak with Dromio since at first
I sent him from the mart. See, here he comes.
    Enter Dromio of Syracuse
How now, sir. Is your merry humour altered?
As you love strokes, so jest with me again.
You know no Centaur. You received no gold.
Your mistress sent to have me home to dinner.   10
My house was at the Phoenix. Wast thou mad
That thus so madly thou didst answer me?

DROMIO OF SYRACUSE

What answer, sir? When spake I such a word?

ANTIPHOLUS OF SYRACUSE

Even now, even here, not half an hour since.

DROMIO OF SYRACUSE

I did not see you since you sent me hence
Home to the Centaur with the gold you gave me.

ANTIPHOLUS OF SYRACUSE

Villain, thou didst deny the gold's receipt,
And toldest me of a mistress and a dinner,
For which I hope thou feltest I was displeased.

DROMIO OF SYRACUSE

I am glad to see you in this merry vein.   20
What means this jest, I pray you, master, tell me?

ANTIPHOLUS OF SYRACUSE

Yea, dost thou jeer and flout me in the teeth?
Thinkest thou I jest? Hold, take thou that, and that.
    He beats Dromio

DROMIO OF SYRACUSE
Hold, sir, for God's sake; now your jest is earnest.
Upon what bargain do you give it me?

ANTIPHOLUS OF SYRACUSE
Because that I familiarly sometimes
Do use you for my fool, and chat with you,
Your sauciness will jest upon my love,
And make a common of my serious hours.
30 When the sun shines let foolish gnats make sport,
But creep in crannies when he hides his beams.
If you will jest with me, know my aspect,
And fashion your demeanour to my looks,
Or I will beat this method in your sconce.

DROMIO OF SYRACUSE 'Sconce' call you it? So you
would leave battering I had rather have it a head. An you
use these blows long I must get a sconce for my head,
and ensconce it too, or else I shall seek my wit in my
shoulders. But I pray, sir, why am I beaten?

40 ANTIPHOLUS OF SYRACUSE Dost thou not know?

DROMIO OF SYRACUSE Nothing, sir, but that I am
beaten.

ANTIPHOLUS OF SYRACUSE Shall I tell you why?

DROMIO OF SYRACUSE Ay, sir, and wherefore; for they
say every why hath a wherefore.

ANTIPHOLUS OF SYRACUSE
Why first: for flouting me; and then wherefore:
For urging it the second time to me.

DROMIO OF SYRACUSE
Was there ever any man thus beaten out of season,
When in the why and the wherefore is neither rhyme nor
reason?
50 Well, sir, I thank you.

ANTIPHOLUS OF SYRACUSE Thank me, sir, for what?

DROMIO OF SYRACUSE Marry, sir, for this something that you gave me for nothing.

ANTIPHOLUS OF SYRACUSE I'll make you amends next, to give you nothing for something. But say, sir, is it dinner-time?

DROMIO OF SYRACUSE No, sir. I think the meat wants that I have.

ANTIPHOLUS OF SYRACUSE In good time, sir. What's that? 60

DROMIO OF SYRACUSE Basting.

ANTIPHOLUS OF SYRACUSE Well, sir, then 'twill be dry.

DROMIO OF SYRACUSE If it be, sir, I pray you eat none of it.

ANTIPHOLUS OF SYRACUSE Your reason?

DROMIO OF SYRACUSE Lest it make you choleric, and purchase me another dry basting.

ANTIPHOLUS OF SYRACUSE Well, sir, learn to jest in good time. There's a time for all things. 70

DROMIO OF SYRACUSE I durst have denied that before you were so choleric.

ANTIPHOLUS OF SYRACUSE By what rule, sir?

DROMIO OF SYRACUSE Marry, sir, by a rule as plain as the plain bald pate of Father Time himself.

ANTIPHOLUS OF SYRACUSE Let's hear it.

DROMIO OF SYRACUSE There's no time for a man to recover his hair that grows bald by nature.

ANTIPHOLUS OF SYRACUSE May he not do it by fine and recovery? 80

DROMIO OF SYRACUSE Yes, to pay a fine for a periwig, and recover the lost hair of another man.

ANTIPHOLUS OF SYRACUSE Why is Time such a niggard of hair, being, as it is, so plentiful an excrement?

DROMIO OF SYRACUSE Because it is a blessing that he bestows on beasts, and what he hath scanted men in hair he hath given them in wit.

ANTIPHOLUS OF SYRACUSE Why, but there's many a man hath more hair than wit.

90 DROMIO OF SYRACUSE Not a man of those but he hath the wit to lose his hair.

ANTIPHOLUS OF SYRACUSE Why, thou didst conclude hairy men plain dealers, without wit.

DROMIO OF SYRACUSE The plainer dealer, the sooner lost. Yet he loseth it in a kind of jollity.

ANTIPHOLUS OF SYRACUSE For what reason?

DROMIO OF SYRACUSE For two, and sound ones, too.

ANTIPHOLUS OF SYRACUSE Nay, not sound, I pray you.

100 DROMIO OF SYRACUSE Sure ones, then.

ANTIPHOLUS OF SYRACUSE Nay, not sure in a thing falsing.

DROMIO OF SYRACUSE Certain ones, then.

ANTIPHOLUS OF SYRACUSE Name them.

DROMIO OF SYRACUSE The one, to save the money that he spends in tiring. The other, that at dinner they should not drop in his porridge.

ANTIPHOLUS OF SYRACUSE You would all this time have proved there is no time for all things.

110 DROMIO OF SYRACUSE Marry, and did, sir; namely, e'en no time to recover hair lost by nature.

ANTIPHOLUS OF SYRACUSE But your reason was not substantial, why there is no time to recover.

DROMIO OF SYRACUSE Thus I mend it: Time himself is bald, and therefore to the world's end will have bald followers.

ANTIPHOLUS OF SYRACUSE I knew 'twould be a bald conclusion. But soft – who wafts us yonder?

Enter Adriana and Luciana

ADRIANA

Ay, ay, Antipholus, look strange and frown.
Some other mistress hath thy sweet aspects.   120
I am not Adriana, nor thy wife.
The time was once when thou unurged wouldst vow
That never words were music to thine ear,
That never object pleasing in thine eye,
That never touch well welcome to thy hand,
That never meat sweet-savoured in thy taste,
Unless I spake, or looked, or touched, or carved to thee.
How comes it now, my husband, O how comes it,
That thou art then estrangèd from thyself?
Thyself I call it, being strange to me   130
That, undividable, incorporate,
Am better than thy dear self's better part.
Ah, do not tear away thyself from me;
For know, my love, as easy mayst thou fall
A drop of water in the breaking gulf,
And take unmingled thence that drop again
Without addition or diminishing,
As take from me thyself, and not me too.
How dearly would it touch thee to the quick
Shouldst thou but hear I were licentious,   140
And that this body consecrate to thee
By ruffian lust should be contaminate?
Wouldst thou not spit at me, and spurn at me,
And hurl the name of husband in my face,
And tear the stained skin off my harlot brow,
And from my false hand cut the wedding ring,
And break it with a deep-divorcing vow?
I know thou canst, and therefore see thou do it!
I am possessed with an adulterate blot.
My blood is mingled with the crime of lust;   150

For if we two be one, and thou play false,
I do digest the poison of thy flesh,
Being strumpeted by thy contagion.
Keep then fair league and truce with thy true bed,
I live unstained, thou undishonourèd.

ANTIPHOLUS OF SYRACUSE
Plead you to me, fair dame? I know you not.
In Ephesus I am but two hours old,
As strange unto your town as to your talk,
Who, every word by all my wit being scanned,
160 Wants wit in all one word to understand.

LUCIANA
Fie, brother, how the world is changed with you.
When were you wont to use my sister thus?
She sent for you by Dromio home to dinner.

ANTIPHOLUS OF SYRACUSE
By Dromio?

DROMIO OF SYRACUSE
By me?

ADRIANA
By thee; and this thou didst return from him:
That he did buffet thee, and in his blows
Denied my house for his, me for his wife.

ANTIPHOLUS OF SYRACUSE
Did you converse, sir, with this gentlewoman?
170 What is the course and drift of your compact?

DROMIO OF SYRACUSE
I, sir? I never saw her till this time.

ANTIPHOLUS OF SYRACUSE
Villain, thou liest; for even her very words
Didst thou deliver to me on the mart.

DROMIO OF SYRACUSE
I never spake with her in all my life.

ANTIPHOLUS OF SYRACUSE

How can she thus then call us by our names? –
Unless it be by inspiration.

ADRIANA

How ill agrees it with your gravity
To counterfeit thus grossly with your slave,
Abetting him to thwart me in my mood.
Be it my wrong you are from me exempt;   180
But wrong not that wrong with a more contempt.
Come, I will fasten on this sleeve of thine.
Thou art an elm, my husband; I a vine,
Whose weakness, married to thy stronger state,
Makes me with thy strength to communicate.
If aught possess thee from me, it is dross,
Usurping ivy, briar, or idle moss,
Who, all for want of pruning, with intrusion
Infect thy sap, and live on thy confusion.

ANTIPHOLUS OF SYRACUSE (*aside*)

To me she speaks; she moves me for her theme.   190
What, was I married to her in my dream?
Or sleep I now, and think I hear all this?
What error drives our eyes and ears amiss?
Until I know this sure uncertainty,
I'll entertain the offered fallacy.

LUCIANA

Dromio, go bid the servants spread for dinner.

DROMIO OF SYRACUSE (*aside*)

O for my beads! I cross me for a sinner.
This is the fairy land. O spite of spites,
We talk with goblins, owls, and sprites.
If we obey them not, this will ensue: 200
They'll suck our breath, or pinch us black and blue.

LUCIANA

Why pratest thou to thyself, and answerest not?

67

Dromio, thou Dromio, thou snail, thou slug, thou sot.

DROMIO OF SYRACUSE

I am transformèd, master, am not I?

ANTIPHOLUS OF SYRACUSE

I think thou art in mind, and so am I.

DROMIO OF SYRACUSE

Nay, master, both in mind and in my shape.

ANTIPHOLUS OF SYRACUSE

Thou hast thine own form.

DROMIO OF SYRACUSE

No, I am an ape.

LUCIANA

If thou art changed to aught, 'tis to an ass.

DROMIO OF SYRACUSE

210   'Tis true, she rides me, and I long for grass.
'Tis so, I am an ass; else it could never be
But I should know her as well as she knows me.

ADRIANA

Come, come, no longer will I be a fool,
To put the finger in the eye and weep
Whilst man and master laughs my woes to scorn.
Come, sir, to dinner. – Dromio, keep the gate. –
Husband, I'll dine above with you today,
And shrive you of a thousand idle pranks. –
Sirrah, if any ask you for your master,

220   Say he dines forth, and let no creature enter. –
Come, sister. – Dromio, play the porter well.

ANTIPHOLUS OF SYRACUSE (*aside*)

Am I in earth, in heaven, or in hell?
Sleeping or waking? mad or well advised?
Known unto these, and to myself disguised!
I'll say as they say, and persever so,
And in this mist at all adventures go.

DROMIO OF SYRACUSE
    Master, shall I be porter at the gate?
ADRIANA
    Ay, and let none enter, lest I break your pate.
LUCIANA
    Come, come, Antipholus, we dine too late.   *Exeunt*

*

Enter Antipholus of Ephesus, his man Dromio, Angelo III.1
the goldsmith, and Balthasar the merchant
ANTIPHOLUS OF EPHESUS
    Good Signor Angelo, you must excuse us all.
    My wife is shrewish when I keep not hours.
    Say that I lingered with you at your shop
    To see the making of her carcanet,
    And that tomorrow you will bring it home.
    But here's a villain that would face me down
    He met me on the mart, and that I beat him,
    And charged him with a thousand marks in gold,
    And that I did deny my wife and house.
    Thou drunkard, thou – what didst thou mean by this? 10
DROMIO OF EPHESUS
    Say what you will, sir, but I know what I know:
    That you beat me at the mart I have your hand to show.
    If the skin were parchment and the blows you gave were
            ink,
    Your own handwriting would tell you what I think.
ANTIPHOLUS OF EPHESUS
    I think thou art an ass.
DROMIO OF EPHESUS   Marry, so it doth appear
    By the wrongs I suffer, and the blows I bear.
    I should kick, being kicked, and, being at that pass,

You would keep from my heels, and beware of an ass.

ANTIPHOLUS OF EPHESUS

You're sad, Signor Balthasar. Pray God our cheer

20   May answer my good will, and your good welcome here.

BALTHASAR

I hold your dainties cheap, sir, and your welcome dear.

ANTIPHOLUS OF EPHESUS

O, Signor Balthasar, either at flesh or fish

A table full of welcome makes scarce one dainty dish.

BALTHASAR

Good meat, sir, is common. That every churl affords.

ANTIPHOLUS OF EPHESUS

And welcome more common, for that's nothing but words.

BALTHASAR

Small cheer and great welcome makes a merry feast.

ANTIPHOLUS OF EPHESUS

Ay, to a niggardly host and more sparing guest.

But though my cates be mean, take them in good part.

Better cheer may you have, but not with better heart.

30   But soft, my door is locked. Go bid them let us in.

DROMIO OF EPHESUS

Maud, Bridget, Marian, Cicely, Gillian, Ginn!

DROMIO OF SYRACUSE (*within*)

Mome, malthorse, capon, coxcomb, idiot, patch,

Either get thee from the door or sit down at the hatch.

Dost thou conjure for wenches, that thou callest for such
    store,

When one is one too many? Go, get thee from the door.

DROMIO OF EPHESUS

What patch is made our porter? – My master stays in
    the street.

DROMIO OF SYRACUSE (*within*)

Let him walk from whence he came, lest he catch cold
    on's feet.

ANTIPHOLUS OF EPHESUS

Who talks within, there? Hoa, open the door.

DROMIO OF SYRACUSE (*within*)

Right, sir, I'll tell you when an you'll tell me wherefore.

ANTIPHOLUS OF EPHESUS

Wherefore? For my dinner. I have not dined today.   40

DROMIO OF SYRACUSE (*within*)

Nor today here you must not. Come again when you may.

ANTIPHOLUS OF EPHESUS

What art thou that keepest me out from the house I
    owe?

DROMIO OF SYRACUSE (*within*)

The porter for this time, sir, and my name is Dromio.

DROMIO OF EPHESUS

O, villain, thou hast stolen both mine office and my
    name.

The one ne'er got me credit, the other mickle blame.

If thou hadst been Dromio today in my place,

Thou wouldst have changed thy face for a name, or thy
    name for an ass.

Enter Luce

LUCE

What a coil is there, Dromio! Who are those at the gate?

DROMIO OF EPHESUS

Let my master in, Luce.

LUCE   Faith, no, he comes too late;

And so tell your master.

DROMIO OF EPHESUS   O lord, I must laugh.   50

Have at you with a proverb: shall I set in my staff?

LUCE

Have at you with another. That's 'When? Can you tell?'

DROMIO OF SYRACUSE (*within*)

If thy name be called Luce, Luce, thou hast answered
    him well.

ANTIPHOLUS OF EPHESUS

Do you hear, you minion? You'll let us in, I trow.

LUCE

I thought to have asked you.

DROMIO OF SYRACUSE (*within*) And you said no.

DROMIO OF EPHESUS

So come – help. Well struck! There was blow for blow.

ANTIPHOLUS OF EPHESUS

Thou baggage, let me in.

LUCE   Can you tell for whose sake?

DROMIO OF EPHESUS

Master, knock the door hard.

LUCE   Let him knock till it ache.

ANTIPHOLUS OF EPHESUS

You'll cry for this, minion, if I beat the door down.

LUCE

60   What needs all that, and a pair of stocks in the town?
        Enter Adriana

ADRIANA

Who is that at the door that keeps all this noise?

DROMIO OF SYRACUSE (*within*)

By my troth, your town is troubled with unruly boys.

ANTIPHOLUS OF EPHESUS

Are you there, wife? You might have come before.

ADRIANA

Your wife, sir knave? Go get you from the door.

                                        Exit with Luce

DROMIO OF EPHESUS

If you went in pain, master, this knave would go sore.

ANGELO

Here is neither cheer, sir, nor welcome. We would fain
        have either.

BALTHASAR

In debating which was best, we shall part with neither.

72

DROMIO OF EPHESUS

They stand at the door, master. Bid them welcome
    hither.

ANTIPHOLUS OF EPHESUS

There is something in the wind, that we cannot get in.

DROMIO OF EPHESUS

You would say so, master, if your garments were thin. 70
Your cake here is warm within. You stand here in the
    cold.
It would make a man mad as a buck to be so bought
    and sold.

ANTIPHOLUS OF EPHESUS

Go fetch me something. I'll break ope the gate.

DROMIO OF SYRACUSE (*within*)

Break any breaking here, and I'll break your knave's
    pate.

DROMIO OF EPHESUS

A man may break a word with you, sir, and words are
    but wind;
Ay, and break it in your face, so he break it not behind.

DROMIO OF SYRACUSE (*within*)

It seems thou wantest breaking. Out upon thee, hind!

DROMIO OF EPHESUS

Here's too much 'Out upon thee.' I pray thee, let me in.

DROMIO OF SYRACUSE (*within*)

Ay, when fowls have no feathers, and fish have no fin.

ANTIPHOLUS OF EPHESUS

Well, I'll break in. Go borrow me a crow. 80

DROMIO OF EPHESUS

A crow without feather, master – mean you so?
For a fish without a fin, there's a fowl without a feather. –
If a crow help us in, sirrah, we'll pluck a crow together.

ANTIPHOLUS OF EPHESUS

Go, get thee gone. Fetch me an iron crow.

BALTHASAR

    Have patience, sir. O, let it not be so.
    Herein you war against your reputation,
    And draw within the compass of suspect
    The unviolated honour of your wife.
    Once this: your long experience of her wisdom,
90   Her sober virtue, years, and modesty,
    Plead on her part some cause to you unknown.
    And doubt not, sir, but she will well excuse
    Why at this time the doors are made against you.
    Be ruled by me. Depart in patience,
    And let us to the Tiger all to dinner,
    And about evening come yourself alone
    To know the reason of this strange restraint.
    If by strong hand you offer to break in
    Now in the stirring passage of the day,
100   A vulgar comment will be made of it,
    And that supposèd by the common rout
    Against your yet ungallèd estimation
    That may with foul intrusion enter in
    And dwell upon your grave when you are dead.
    For slander lives upon succession,
    For ever housed where it gets possession.

ANTIPHOLUS OF EPHESUS

    You have prevailed. I will depart in quiet,
    And in despite of mirth mean to be merry.
    I know a wench of excellent discourse,
110   Pretty and witty; wild, and yet, too, gentle.
    There will we dine. This woman that I mean,
    My wife – but, I protest, without desert –
    Hath oftentimes upbraided me withal.
    To her will we to dinner. (*To Angelo*) Get you home
    And fetch the chain. By this, I know, 'tis made.
    Bring it, I pray you, to the Porpentine,

For there's the house. That chain will I bestow –
Be it for nothing but to spite my wife –
Upon mine hostess there. Good sir, make haste.
Since mine own doors refuse to entertain me,   120
I'll knock elsewhere to see if they'll disdain me.

ANGELO

I'll meet you at that place some hour hence.

ANTIPHOLUS OF EPHESUS

Do so. – This jest shall cost me some expense.

Exeunt

Enter Luciana with Antipholus of Syracuse   III.2

LUCIANA

And may it be that you have quite forgot
    A husband's office? Shall, Antipholus,
Even in the spring of love thy love-springs rot?
    Shall love in building grow so ruinous?
If you did wed my sister for her wealth,
    Then for her wealth's sake use her with more
        kindness;
Or if you like elsewhere, do it by stealth –
    Muffle your false love with some show of blindness.
Let not my sister read it in your eye.
    Be not thy tongue thy own shame's orator.   10
Look sweet, speak fair, become disloyalty.
    Apparel vice like virtue's harbinger.
Bear a fair presence, though your heart be tainted;
    Teach sin the carriage of a holy saint;
Be secret-false – what need she be acquainted?
    What simple thief brags of his own attaint?
'Tis double wrong to truant with your bed
    And let her read it in thy looks at board.
Shame hath a bastard fame, well managèd;

75

20 Ill deeds is doubled with an evil word.
Alas, poor women, make us but believe –
  Being compact of credit – that you love us.
Though others have the arm, show us the sleeve.
  We in your motion turn, and you may move us.
Then, gentle brother, get you in again.
  Comfort my sister, cheer her, call her wife.
'Tis holy sport to be a little vain
  When the sweet breath of flattery conquers strife.

ANTIPHOLUS OF SYRACUSE

Sweet mistress, what your name is else I know not,
30 Nor by what wonder you do hit of mine.
Less in your knowledge and your grace you show not
  Than our earth's wonder, more than earth divine.
Teach me, dear creature, how to think and speak.
  Lay open to my earthy gross conceit,
Smothered in errors, feeble, shallow, weak,
  The folded meaning of your words' deceit.
Against my soul's pure truth why labour you
  To make it wander in an unknown field?
Are you a god? Would you create me new?
40 Transform me, then, and to your power I'll yield.
But if that I am I, then well I know
  Your weeping sister is no wife of mine,
Nor to her bed no homage do I owe.
  Far more, far more to you do I decline.
O, train me not, sweet mermaid, with thy note
  To drown me in thy sister's flood of tears.
Sing, siren, for thyself, and I will dote.
  Spread o'er the silver waves thy golden hairs
And as a bed I'll take thee, and there lie,
50 And in that glorious supposition think
He gains by death that hath such means to die.
  Let love, being light, be drownèd if she sink.

76

LUCIANA

What, are you mad, that you do reason so?

ANTIPHOLUS OF SYRACUSE

Not mad, but mated. How I do not know.

LUCIANA

It is a fault that springeth from your eye.

ANTIPHOLUS OF SYRACUSE

For gazing on your beams, fair sun, being by.

LUCIANA

Gaze where you should, and that will clear your sight.

ANTIPHOLUS OF SYRACUSE

As good to wink, sweet love, as look on night.

LUCIANA

Why call you me 'love'? Call my sister so.

ANTIPHOLUS OF SYRACUSE

Thy sister's sister.

LUCIANA   That's my sister.

ANTIPHOLUS OF SYRACUSE   No,   60
It is thyself, mine own self's better part,
Mine eye's clear eye, my dear heart's dearer heart,
My food, my fortune, and my sweet hope's aim,
My sole earth's heaven, and my heaven's claim.

LUCIANA

All this my sister is, or else should be.

ANTIPHOLUS OF SYRACUSE

Call thyself sister, sweet, for I am thee.
Thee will I love, and with thee lead my life.
Thou hast no husband yet, nor I no wife.
Give me thy hand.

LUCIANA   O soft, sir, hold you still.
I'll fetch my sister to get her good will.   *Exit* 70
    Enter Dromio of Syracuse

ANTIPHOLUS OF SYRACUSE Why, how now, Dromio.
Where runnest thou so fast?

DROMIO OF SYRACUSE Do you know me, sir? Am I Dromio? Am I your man? Am I myself?

ANTIPHOLUS OF SYRACUSE Thou art, Dromio. Thou art my man, thou art thyself.

DROMIO OF SYRACUSE I am an ass, I am a woman's man, and besides myself.

ANTIPHOLUS OF SYRACUSE What woman's man? And
80 how besides thyself?

DROMIO OF SYRACUSE Marry, sir, besides myself I am due to a woman. One that claims me, one that haunts me, one that will have me.

ANTIPHOLUS OF SYRACUSE What claim lays she to thee?

DROMIO OF SYRACUSE Marry, sir, such claim as you would lay to your horse; and she would have me as a beast – not that, I being a beast, she would have me, but that she, being a very beastly creature, lays claim
90 to me.

ANTIPHOLUS OF SYRACUSE What is she?

DROMIO OF SYRACUSE A very reverend body – ay, such a one as a man may not speak of without he say 'sir-reverence'. I have but lean luck in the match, and yet is she a wondrous fat marriage.

ANTIPHOLUS OF SYRACUSE How dost thou mean, a fat marriage?

DROMIO OF SYRACUSE Marry, sir, she's the kitchen wench, and all grease; and I know not what use to put
100 her to but to make a lamp of her and run from her by her own light. I warrant her rags and the tallow in them will burn a Poland winter. If she lives till dooms-day she'll burn a week longer than the whole world.

ANTIPHOLUS OF SYRACUSE What complexion is she of?

DROMIO OF SYRACUSE Swart like my shoe, but her face

nothing like so clean kept. For why? She sweats a man may go overshoes in the grime of it.

ANTIPHOLUS OF SYRACUSE That's a fault that water will mend. 110

DROMIO OF SYRACUSE No, sir, 'tis in grain. Noah's flood could not do it.

ANTIPHOLUS OF SYRACUSE What's her name?

DROMIO OF SYRACUSE Nell, sir. But her name and three quarters – that's an ell and three quarters – will not measure her from hip to hip.

ANTIPHOLUS OF SYRACUSE Then she bears some breadth?

DROMIO OF SYRACUSE No longer from head to foot than from hip to hip. She is spherical, like a globe. I 120 could find out countries in her.

ANTIPHOLUS OF SYRACUSE In what part of her body stands Ireland?

DROMIO OF SYRACUSE Marry, sir, in her buttocks. I found it out by the bogs.

ANTIPHOLUS OF SYRACUSE Where Scotland?

DROMIO OF SYRACUSE I found it by the barrenness, hard in the palm of the hand.

ANTIPHOLUS OF SYRACUSE Where France?

DROMIO OF SYRACUSE In her forehead, armed and 130 reverted, making war against her heir.

ANTIPHOLUS OF SYRACUSE Where England?

DROMIO OF SYRACUSE I looked for the chalky cliffs, but I could find no whiteness in them. But I guess it stood in her chin, by the salt rheum that ran between France and it.

ANTIPHOLUS OF SYRACUSE Where Spain?

DROMIO OF SYRACUSE Faith, I saw it not, but I felt it hot in her breath.

ANTIPHOLUS OF SYRACUSE Where America, the Indies? 140

DROMIO OF SYRACUSE O, sir, upon her nose, all o'er
embellished with rubies, carbuncles, sapphires, declining their rich aspect to the hot breath of Spain, who
sent whole armadoes of carracks to be ballast at her nose.

ANTIPHOLUS OF SYRACUSE Where stood Belgia, the
Netherlands?

DROMIO OF SYRACUSE O, sir, I did not look so low.
To conclude, this drudge or diviner laid claim to me,
called me Dromio, swore I was assured to her, told me
150   what privy marks I had about me, as the mark of my
shoulder, the mole in my neck, the great wart on my
left arm, that I, amazed, ran from her as a witch.
And I think if my breast had not been made of faith
    and my heart of steel,
She had transformed me to a curtal dog, and made me
    turn i'the wheel.

ANTIPHOLUS OF SYRACUSE
Go, hie thee presently. Post to the road.
An if the wind blow any way from shore
I will not harbour in this town tonight.
If any bark put forth, come to the mart,
Where I will walk till thou return to me.
160 If everyone knows us, and we know none,
'Tis time, I think, to trudge, pack, and be gone.

DROMIO OF SYRACUSE
As from a bear a man would run for life,
So fly I from her that would be my wife.   *Exit*

ANTIPHOLUS OF SYRACUSE
There's none but witches do inhabit here,
And therefore 'tis high time that I were hence.
She that doth call me husband, even my soul
Doth for a wife abhor. But her fair sister,
Possessed with such a gentle sovereign grace,
Of such enchanting presence and discourse,

Hath almost made me traitor to myself. 170
But lest myself be guilty to self-wrong,
I'll stop mine ears against the mermaid's song.
Enter Angelo, with the chain

ANGELO
Master Antipholus.

ANTIPHOLUS OF SYRACUSE
              Ay, that's my name.

ANGELO
I know it well, sir. Lo, here's the chain.
I thought to have ta'en you at the Porpentine.
The chain unfinished made me stay thus long.

ANTIPHOLUS OF SYRACUSE
What is your will that I shall do with this?

ANGELO
What please yourself, sir. I have made it for you.

ANTIPHOLUS OF SYRACUSE
Made it for me, sir? I bespoke it not.

ANGELO
Not once, nor twice, but twenty times you have. 180
Go home with it, and please your wife withal,
And soon at supper-time I'll visit you,
And then receive my money for the chain.

ANTIPHOLUS OF SYRACUSE
I pray you, sir, receive the money now,
For fear you ne'er see chain nor money more.

ANGELO
You are a merry man, sir. Fare you well. *Exit*

ANTIPHOLUS OF SYRACUSE
What I should think of this I cannot tell.
But this I think: there's no man is so vain
That would refuse so fair an offered chain.
I see a man here needs not live by shifts, 190
When in the streets he meets such golden gifts.

I'll to the mart, and there for Dromio stay;
If any ship put out, then straight away!   *Ex*

＊

IV.1   *Enter Second Merchant, Angelo the goldsmith, an*
             an Officer

SECOND MERCHANT
You know since Pentecost the sum is due,
And since I have not much importuned you;
Nor now I had not, but that I am bound
To Persia, and want guilders for my voyage.
Therefore make present satisfaction,
Or I'll attach you by this officer.

ANGELO
Even just the sum that I do owe to you
Is growing to me by Antipholus,
And in the instant that I met with you
10   He had of me a chain. At five o'clock
I shall receive the money for the same.
Pleaseth you walk with me down to his house,
I will discharge my bond, and thank you, too.
             Enter Antipholus of Ephesus and Dromio of Ephesus
             from the Courtesan's

OFFICER
That labour may you save. See where he comes.

ANTIPHOLUS OF EPHESUS
While I go to the goldsmith's house, go thou
And buy a rope's end; that will I bestow
Among my wife and her confederates
For locking me out of my doors by day.
But soft, I see the goldsmith. Get thee gone.
20   Buy thou a rope, and bring it home to me.

DROMIO OF EPHESUS
    I buy a thousand pound a year, I buy a rope.   *Exit*
ANTIPHOLUS OF EPHESUS
    A man is well holp up that trusts to you.
    I promisèd your presence and the chain,
    But neither chain nor goldsmith came to me.
    Belike you thought our love would last too long
    If it were chained together, and therefore came not.
ANGELO
    Saving your merry humour, here's the note
    How much your chain weighs to the utmost carat,
    The fineness of the gold, and chargeful fashion,
    Which doth amount to three odd ducats more   30
    Than I stand debted to this gentleman.
    I pray you see him presently discharged,
    For he is bound to sea, and stays but for it.
ANTIPHOLUS OF EPHESUS
    I am not furnished with the present money;
    Besides, I have some business in the town.
    Good signor, take the stranger to my house,
    And with you take the chain, and bid my wife
    Disburse the sum on the receipt thereof.
    Perchance I will be there as soon as you.
ANGELO
    Then you will bring the chain to her yourself.   40
ANTIPHOLUS OF EPHESUS
    No, bear it with you lest I come not time enough.
ANGELO
    Well, sir, I will. Have you the chain about you?
ANTIPHOLUS OF EPHESUS
    An if I have not, sir, I hope you have;
    Or else you may return without your money.
ANGELO
    Nay, come, I pray you, sir, give me the chain.

Both wind and tide stays for this gentleman,
And I, too blame, have held him here too long.

ANTIPHOLUS OF EPHESUS

Good Lord! You use this dalliance to excuse
Your breach of promise to the Porpentine.

50 I should have chid you for not bringing it,
But like a shrew you first begin to brawl.

SECOND MERCHANT

The hour steals on. I pray you, sir, dispatch.

ANGELO

You hear how he importunes me. The chain!

ANTIPHOLUS OF EPHESUS

Why, give it to my wife, and fetch your money.

ANGELO

Come, come. You know I gave it you even now.
Either send the chain, or send me by some token.

ANTIPHOLUS OF EPHESUS

Fie, now you run this humour out of breath.
Come, where's the chain? I pray you let me see it.

SECOND MERCHANT

My business cannot brook this dalliance.

60 Good sir, say whe'er you'll answer me or no.
If not, I'll leave him to the officer.

ANTIPHOLUS OF EPHESUS

I answer you? What should I answer you?

ANGELO

The money that you owe me for the chain.

ANTIPHOLUS OF EPHESUS

I owe you none till I receive the chain.

ANGELO

You know I gave it you half an hour since.

ANTIPHOLUS OF EPHESUS

You gave me none. You wrong me much to say so.

ANGELO

You wrong me more, sir, in denying it.
Consider how it stands upon my credit.

SECOND MERCHANT

Well, officer, arrest him at my suit.

OFFICER

I do,   70
And charge you in the Duke's name to obey me.

ANGELO

This touches me in reputation.
Either consent to pay this sum for me,
Or I attach you by this officer.

ANTIPHOLUS OF EPHESUS

Consent to pay thee that I never had?
Arrest me, foolish fellow, if thou darest.

ANGELO

Here is thy fee – arrest him, officer.
I would not spare my brother in this case
If he should scorn me so apparently.

OFFICER

I do arrest you, sir. You hear the suit.   80

ANTIPHOLUS OF EPHESUS

I do obey thee till I give thee bail.
But, sirrah, you shall buy this sport as dear
As all the metal in your shop will answer.

ANGELO

Sir, sir, I shall have law in Ephesus,
To your notorious shame, I doubt it not.
Enter Dromio of Syracuse, from the bay

DROMIO OF SYRACUSE

Master, there's a bark of Epidamnum
That stays but till her owner comes aboard,
And then she bears away. Our fraughtage, sir,
I have conveyed aboard, and I have bought

90 The oil, the balsamum, and aqua-vitae.
The ship is in her trim; the merry wind
Blows fair from land. They stay for naught at all
But for their owner, master, and yourself.

ANTIPHOLUS OF EPHESUS

How now? A madman? Why, thou peevish sheep,
What ship of Epidamnum stays for me?

DROMIO OF SYRACUSE

A ship you sent me to, to hire waftage.

ANTIPHOLUS OF EPHESUS

Thou drunken slave, I sent thee for a rope,
And told thee to what purpose, and what end.

DROMIO OF SYRACUSE

You sent me for a rope's end as soon.
100 You sent me to the bay, sir, for a bark.

ANTIPHOLUS OF EPHESUS

I will debate this matter at more leisure,
And teach your ears to list me with more heed.
To Adriana, villain, hie thee straight.
Give her this key, and tell her in the desk
That's covered o'er with Turkish tapestry
There is a purse of ducats. Let her send it.
Tell her I am arrested in the street,
And that shall bail me. Hie thee, slave. Be gone.
On, officer; to prison, till it come.

Exeunt all but Dromio of Syracuse

DROMIO OF SYRACUSE

110 To Adriana. That is where we dined,
Where Dowsabel did claim me for her husband.
She is too big, I hope, for me to compass.
Thither I must, although against my will;
For servants must their masters' minds fulfil. *Exit*

ADRIANA

Ah, Luciana, did he tempt thee so?
  Mightst thou perceive austerely in his eye
That he did plead in earnest, yea or no?
  Looked he or red or pale, or sad or merrily?
What observation madest thou in this case
Of his heart's meteors tilting in his face?

LUCIANA

First, he denied you had in him no right.

ADRIANA

He meant he did me none, the more my spite.

LUCIANA

Then swore he that he was a stranger here.

ADRIANA

And true he swore, though yet forsworn he were.   10

LUCIANA

Then pleaded I for you.

ADRIANA   And what said he?

LUCIANA

That love I begged for you, he begged of me.

ADRIANA

With what persuasion did he tempt thy love?

LUCIANA

With words that in an honest suit might move.
First he did praise my beauty, then my speech.

ADRIANA

Didst speak him fair?

LUCIANA   Have patience, I beseech.

ADRIANA

I cannot nor I will not hold me still.
My tongue, though not my heart, shall have his will.
He is deformèd, crooked, old, and sere;
Ill-faced, worse-bodied, shapeless everywhere;   20

87

Vicious, ungentle, foolish, blunt, unkind,
Stigmatical in making, worse in mind.

LUCIANA
Who would be jealous, then, of such a one?
No evil lost is wailed when it is gone.

ADRIANA
Ah, but I think him better than I say,
And yet would herein others' eyes were worse.
Far from her nest the lapwing cries away.
My heart prays for him, though my tongue do curse.
Enter Dromio of Syracuse

DROMIO OF SYRACUSE
Here, go – the desk, the purse, sweet, now, make haste.

LUCIANA
30   How hast thou lost thy breath?

DROMIO OF SYRACUSE   By running fast.

ADRIANA
Where is thy master, Dromio? Is he well?

DROMIO OF SYRACUSE
No. He's in Tartar limbo, worse than hell.
A devil in an everlasting garment hath him,
One whose hard heart is buttoned up with steel,
A fiend, a fairy, pitiless and rough;
A wolf, nay, worse, a fellow all in buff;
A backfriend, a shoulder-clapper, one that countermands
The passages of alleys, creeks, and narrow lands;
A hound that runs counter, and yet draws dryfoot well;
40   One that before the Judgement carries poor souls to hell.

ADRIANA
Why, man, what is the matter?

DROMIO OF SYRACUSE
I do not know the matter, he is 'rested on the case.

ADRIANA
What, is he arrested? Tell me at whose suit.

DROMIO OF SYRACUSE

   I know not at whose suit he is arrested well;

   But is in a suit of buff which 'rested him, that can I tell.

   Will you send him, mistress, redemption – the money in
       his desk?

ADRIANA

   Go fetch it, sister.   *Exit Luciana*

            This I wonder at,

   That he unknown to me should be in debt.

   Tell me, was he arrested on a band?

DROMIO OF SYRACUSE

   Not on a band, but on a stronger thing: 50

   A chain, a chain – do you not hear it ring?

ADRIANA

   What, the chain?

DROMIO OF SYRACUSE No, no – the bell. 'Tis time that
       I were gone.

   It was two ere I left him, and now the clock strikes one.

ADRIANA

   The hours come back – that did I never hear.

DROMIO OF SYRACUSE

   O yes, if any hour meet a sergeant 'a turns back for
      very fear.

ADRIANA

   As if time were in debt. How fondly dost thou reason!

DROMIO OF SYRACUSE

   Time is a very bankrupt, and owes more than he's
      worth to season.

   Nay, he's a thief, too. Have you not heard men say

   That time comes stealing on by night and day?

   If 'a be in debt and theft, and a sergeant in the way,   60

   Hath he not reason to turn back an hour in a day?

     Enter Luciana with the money

ADRIANA

Go, Dromio, there's the money. Bear it straight,
   And bring thy master home immediately.
Come, sister, I am pressed down with conceit –
   Conceit, my comfort and my injury.   *Exeunt*

IV.3   *Enter Antipholus of Syracuse*

ANTIPHOLUS OF SYRACUSE

There's not a man I meet but doth salute me
As if I were their well-acquainted friend,
And everyone doth call me by my name.
Some tender money to me, some invite me,
Some other give me thanks for kindness.
Some offer me commodities to buy.
Even now a tailor called me in his shop
And showed me silks that he had bought for me,
And therewithal took measure of my body.
10   Sure, these are but imaginary wiles,
And Lapland sorcerers inhabit here.
          Enter Dromio of Syracuse

DROMIO OF SYRACUSE Master, here's the gold you sent
me for. – What, have you got the picture of old Adam
new-apparelled?

ANTIPHOLUS OF SYRACUSE

What gold is this? What Adam dost thou mean?

DROMIO OF SYRACUSE Not that Adam that kept the
paradise, but that Adam that keeps the prison. He that
goes in the calf's skin that was killed for the prodigal.
He that came behind you, sir, like an evil angel, and bid
20   you forsake your liberty.

ANTIPHOLUS OF SYRACUSE I understand thee not.

DROMIO OF SYRACUSE No? Why, 'tis a plain case: he
that went like a bass viol in a case of leather; the man,

sir, that when gentlemen are tired gives them a sob and
rests them; he, sir, that takes pity on decayed men and
gives them suits of durance; he that sets up his rest to
do more exploits with his mace than a morris-pike.

ANTIPHOLUS OF SYRACUSE What, thou meanest an
officer?

DROMIO OF SYRACUSE Ay, sir, the sergeant of the band 30
– he that brings any man to answer it that breaks his
band; one that thinks a man always going to bed, and
says 'God give you good rest.'

ANTIPHOLUS OF SYRACUSE Well, sir, there rest in
your foolery. Is there any ships puts forth tonight?
May we be gone?

DROMIO OF SYRACUSE Why, sir, I brought you word
an hour since that the bark *Expedition* put forth tonight,
and then were you hindered by the sergeant to tarry for
the hoy *Delay*. Here are the angels that you sent for to 40
deliver you.

ANTIPHOLUS OF SYRACUSE
The fellow is distract, and so am I,
And here we wander in illusions.
Some blessed power deliver us from hence!
    Enter a Courtesan

COURTESAN
Well met, well met, Master Antipholus.
I see, sir, you have found the goldsmith now.
Is that the chain you promised me today?

ANTIPHOLUS OF SYRACUSE
Satan, avoid! I charge thee, tempt me not!

DROMIO OF SYRACUSE Master, is this Mistress Satan?

ANTIPHOLUS OF SYRACUSE It is the devil. 50

DROMIO OF SYRACUSE Nay, she is worse, she is the
devil's dam; and here she comes in the habit of a light
wench; and thereof comes that the wenches say 'God

damn me' – that's as much to say 'God make me a light wench.' It is written they appear to men like angels of light. Light is an effect of fire, and fire will burn. Ergo, light wenches will burn. Come not near her.

COURTESAN
Your man and you are marvellous merry, sir.
Will you go with me? We'll mend our dinner here.

60 DROMIO OF SYRACUSE Master, if you do, expect spoon-meat, or bespeak a long spoon.

ANTIPHOLUS OF SYRACUSE Why, Dromio?

DROMIO OF SYRACUSE Marry, he must have a long spoon that must eat with the devil.

ANTIPHOLUS OF SYRACUSE (to Courtesan)
Avoid then, fiend. What tellest thou me of supping?
Thou art, as you are all, a sorceress.
I conjure thee to leave me and be gone.

COURTESAN
Give me the ring of mine you had at dinner,
Or for my diamond the chain you promised,
70 And I'll be gone, sir, and not trouble you.

DROMIO OF SYRACUSE
Some devils ask but the parings of one's nail,
A rush, a hair, a drop of blood, a pin,
A nut, a cherry stone.
But she, more covetous, would have a chain.
Master, be wise; an if you give it her,
The devil will shake her chain, and fright us with it.

COURTESAN
I pray you, sir, my ring, or else the chain!
I hope you do not mean to cheat me so.

ANTIPHOLUS OF SYRACUSE
Avaunt, thou witch! Come, Dromio, let us go.

DROMIO OF SYRACUSE
80 'Fly pride', says the peacock. Mistress, that you know.

Exeunt Antipholus of Syracuse and
Dromio of Syracuse

COURTESAN

Now, out of doubt, Antipholus is mad,
Else would he never so demean himself.
A ring he hath of mine worth forty ducats,
And for the same he promised me a chain.
Both one and other he denies me now.
The reason that I gather he is mad,
Besides this present instance of his rage,
Is a mad tale he told today at dinner
Of his own doors being shut against his entrance.
Belike his wife, acquainted with his fits,   90
On purpose shut the doors against his way.
My way is now to hie home to his house
And tell his wife that, being lunatic,
He rushed into my house and took perforce
My ring away. This course I fittest choose,
For forty ducats is too much to lose.   *Exit*

Enter Antipholus of Ephesus with the Officer   IV.4

ANTIPHOLUS OF EPHESUS

Fear me not, man. I will not break away.
I'll give thee ere I leave thee so much money
To warrant thee as I am 'rested for.
My wife is in a wayward mood today,
And will not lightly trust the messenger
That I should be attached in Ephesus.
I tell you, 'twill sound harshly in her ears.
    Enter Dromio of Ephesus, with a rope's end
Here comes my man. I think he brings the money.
How now, sir. Have you that I sent you for?

93

DROMIO OF EPHESUS

10   Here's that, I warrant you, will pay them all.

ANTIPHOLUS OF EPHESUS

But where's the money?

DROMIO OF EPHESUS

Why, sir, I gave the money for the rope.

ANTIPHOLUS OF EPHESUS

Five hundred ducats, villain, for a rope?

DROMIO OF EPHESUS

I'll serve you, sir, five hundred at the rate.

ANTIPHOLUS OF EPHESUS

To what end did I bid thee hie thee home?

DROMIO OF EPHESUS

To a rope's end, sir, and to that end am I returned.

ANTIPHOLUS OF EPHESUS

And to that end, sir, I will welcome you.

He beats Dromio

OFFICER

Good sir, be patient.

DROMIO OF EPHESUS

Nay, 'tis for me to be patient. I am in adversity.

OFFICER

20   Good now, hold thy tongue.

DROMIO OF EPHESUS

Nay, rather persuade him to hold his hands.

ANTIPHOLUS OF EPHESUS Thou whoreson, senseless villain.

DROMIO OF EPHESUS I would I were senseless, sir, that I might not feel your blows.

ANTIPHOLUS OF EPHESUS

Thou art sensible in nothing but blows; and so is an ass.

DROMIO OF EPHESUS I am an ass, indeed. You may prove it by my long ears. I have served him from the hour of my nativity to this instant, and have nothing at

his hands for my service but blows. When I am cold, he 30
heats me with beating. When I am warm, he cools me
with beating. I am waked with it when I sleep, raised
with it when I sit, driven out of doors with it when I
go from home, welcomed home with it when I return;
nay, I bear it on my shoulders, as a beggar wont her
brat, and I think when he hath lamed me, I shall beg
with it from door to door.

*Enter Adriana, Luciana, the Courtesan, and a school-
master called Pinch*

ANTIPHOLUS OF EPHESUS
Come, go along – my wife is coming yonder.
DROMIO OF EPHESUS Mistress, *respice finem* – 'respect
your end', or rather, to prophesy like the parrot, 'beware 40
the rope's end'.
ANTIPHOLUS OF EPHESUS
Wilt thou still talk?
He beats Dromio
COURTESAN
How say you now? Is not your husband mad?
ADRIANA
His incivility confirms no less.
Good Doctor Pinch, you are a conjuror.
Establish him in his true sense again,
And I will please you what you will demand.
LUCIANA
Alas, how fiery and how sharp he looks!
COURTESAN
Mark how he trembles in his ecstasy.
PINCH
Give me your hand, and let me feel your pulse. 50
ANTIPHOLUS OF EPHESUS
There is my hand, and let it feel your ear.
He strikes Pinch

IV.4

PINCH

I charge thee, Satan, housed within this man,
To yield possession to my holy prayers,
And to thy state of darkness hie thee straight.
I conjure thee by all the saints in heaven.

ANTIPHOLUS OF EPHESUS

Peace, doting wizard, peace. I am not mad.

ADRIANA

O that thou wert not, poor distressèd soul!

ANTIPHOLUS OF EPHESUS

You minion, you, are these your customers?
Did this companion with the saffron face
60   Revel and feast it at my house today,
Whilst upon me the guilty doors were shut,
And I denied to enter in my house?

ADRIANA

O, husband, God doth know you dined at home,
Where would you had remained until this time,
Free from these slanders and this open shame.

ANTIPHOLUS OF EPHESUS

Dined at home? (*To Dromio*) Thou villain, what sayst
    thou?

DROMIO OF EPHESUS

Sir, sooth to say, you did not dine at home.

ANTIPHOLUS OF EPHESUS

Were not my doors locked up, and I shut out?

DROMIO OF EPHESUS

Perdie, your doors were locked, and you shut out.

ANTIPHOLUS OF EPHESUS

70   And did not she herself revile me there?

DROMIO OF EPHESUS

Sans fable, she herself reviled you there.

ANTIPHOLUS OF EPHESUS

Did not her kitchen-maid rail, taunt, and scorn me?

96

DROMIO OF EPHESUS

Certes she did. The kitchen vestal scorned you.

ANTIPHOLUS OF EPHESUS

And did not I in rage depart from thence?

DROMIO OF EPHESUS

In verity you did. My bones bears witness,
That since have felt the vigour of his rage.

ADRIANA

Is't good to soothe him in these contraries?

PINCH

It is no shame. The fellow finds his vein,
And, yielding to him, humours well his frenzy.

ANTIPHOLUS OF EPHESUS

Thou hast suborned the goldsmith to arrest me.   80

ADRIANA

Alas, I sent you money to redeem you,
By Dromio here, who came in haste for it.

DROMIO OF EPHESUS

Money by me? Heart and good will you might,
But surely, master, not a rag of money.

ANTIPHOLUS OF EPHESUS

Went'st not thou to her for a purse of ducats?

ADRIANA

He came to me, and I delivered it.

LUCIANA

And I am witness with her that she did.

DROMIO OF EPHESUS

God and the ropemaker bear me witness
That I was sent for nothing but a rope.

PINCH

Mistress, both man and master is possessed.   90
I know it by their pale and deadly looks.
They must be bound and laid in some dark room.

ANTIPHOLUS OF EPHESUS (*to Adriana*)
Say, wherefore didst thou lock me forth today,
(*to Dromio of Ephesus*)
And why dost thou deny the bag of gold?

ADRIANA
I did not, gentle husband, lock thee forth.

DROMIO OF EPHESUS
And, gentle master, I received no gold.
But I confess, sir, that we were locked out.

ADRIANA
Dissembling villain, thou speakest false in both.

ANTIPHOLUS OF EPHESUS
Dissembling harlot, thou art false in all,
And art confederate with a damnèd pack
To make a loathsome abject scorn of me.
But with these nails I'll pluck out these false eyes
That would behold in me this shameful sport.

100

ADRIANA
O, bind him, bind him, let him not come near me!
Enter three or four and offer to bind him.
He strives

PINCH
More company! The fiend is strong within him.

LUCIANA
Ay me, poor man, how pale and wan he looks.

ANTIPHOLUS OF EPHESUS
What, will you murder me? Thou, gaoler, thou,
I am thy prisoner – wilt thou suffer them
To make a rescue?

OFFICER   Masters, let him go.
He is my prisoner, and you shall not have him.

110

PINCH
Go bind his man, for he is frantic too.
Dromio is bound

98

ADRIANA

What wilt thou do, thou peevish officer?
Hast thou delight to see a wretched man
Do outrage and displeasure to himself?

OFFICER

He is my prisoner. If I let him go
The debt he owes will be required of me.

ADRIANA

I will discharge thee ere I go from thee.
Bear me forthwith unto his creditor,
And, knowing how the debt grows, I will pay it.
Good Master Doctor, see him safe conveyed   120
Home to my house. O most unhappy day!

ANTIPHOLUS OF EPHESUS

O most unhappy strumpet!

DROMIO OF EPHESUS

Master, I am here entered in bond for you.

ANTIPHOLUS OF EPHESUS

Out on thee, villain! Wherefore dost thou mad me?

DROMIO OF EPHESUS

Will you be bound for nothing? Be mad, good master –
Cry 'the devil!'.

LUCIANA

God help, poor souls, how idly do they talk!

ADRIANA

Go bear him hence. Sister, go you with me.
          Exeunt Pinch and his assistants carrying off
          Antipholus of Ephesus and Dromio of Ephesus. The
          Officer, Adriana, Luciana, and the Courtesan remain
Say now, whose suit is he arrested at?

OFFICER

One Angelo, a goldsmith. Do you know him?   130

ADRIANA

I know the man. What is the sum he owes?

OFFICER
Two hundred ducats.

ADRIANA   Say, how grows it due?

OFFICER
Due for a chain your husband had of him.

ADRIANA
He did bespeak a chain for me, but had it not.

COURTESAN
Whenas your husband all in rage today
Came to my house and took away my ring,
The ring I saw upon his finger now,
Straight after did I meet him with a chain.

ADRIANA
It may be so, but I did never see it.

140 Come, gaoler, bring me where the goldsmith is.
I long to know the truth hereof at large.

Enter Antipholus of Syracuse and Dromio of Syra-
cuse, with their rapiers drawn

LUCIANA
God, for thy mercy, they are loose again!

ADRIANA
And come with naked swords. Let's call more help
To have them bound again.

OFFICER   Away, they'll kill us!

Run all out as fast as may be, frighted

ANTIPHOLUS OF SYRACUSE
I see these witches are afraid of swords.

DROMIO OF SYRACUSE
She that would be your wife now ran from you.

ANTIPHOLUS OF SYRACUSE
Come to the Centaur. Fetch our stuff from thence.
I long that we were safe and sound aboard.

DROMIO OF SYRACUSE Faith, stay here this night. They
150 will surely do us no harm. You saw they speak us fair,

give us gold. Methinks they are such a gentle nation
that but for the mountain of mad flesh that claims
marriage of me, I could find in my heart to stay here
still, and turn witch.

ANTIPHOLUS OF SYRACUSE

I will not stay tonight for all the town;
Therefore away, to get our stuff aboard.   *Exeunt*

✳

Enter Second Merchant and Angelo the goldsmith   V.1

ANGELO

I am sorry, sir, that I have hindered you,
But I protest he had the chain of me,
Though most dishonestly he doth deny it.

SECOND MERCHANT

How is the man esteemed here in the city?

ANGELO

Of very reverend reputation, sir,
Of credit infinite, highly beloved,
Second to none that lives here in the city.
His word might bear my wealth at any time.

SECOND MERCHANT

Speak softly. Yonder, as I think, he walks.
     *Enter Antipholus of Syracuse and Dromio of Syra-
     cuse again*

ANGELO

'Tis so; and that self chain about his neck   10
Which he forswore most monstrously to have.
Good sir, draw near to me. I'll speak to him.
Signor Antipholus, I wonder much
That you would put me to this shame and trouble,
And not without some scandal to yourself,

With circumstance and oaths so to deny
This chain, which now you wear so openly.
Beside the charge, the shame, imprisonment,
You have done wrong to this my honest friend,
Who, but for staying on our controversy,
Had hoisted sail and put to sea today.
This chain you had of me. Can you deny it?

ANTIPHOLUS OF SYRACUSE

I think I had. I never did deny it.

SECOND MERCHANT

Yes, that you did, sir, and forswore it, too.

ANTIPHOLUS OF SYRACUSE

Who heard me to deny it or forswear it?

SECOND MERCHANT

These ears of mine, thou knowest, did hear thee.
Fie on thee, wretch. 'Tis pity that thou livest
To walk where any honest men resort.

ANTIPHOLUS OF SYRACUSE

Thou art a villain to impeach me thus.
I'll prove mine honour and mine honesty
Against thee presently, if thou darest stand.

SECOND MERCHANT

I dare, and do defy thee for a villain.

They draw

Enter Adriana, Luciana, the Courtesan, and others

ADRIANA

Hold, hurt him not, for God's sake; he is mad.
Some get within him, take his sword away.
Bind Dromio too, and bear them to my house.

DROMIO OF SYRACUSE

Run, master, run! For God's sake take a house.
This is some priory. In, or we are spoiled.

*Exeunt Antipholus of Syracuse and Dromio of
Syracuse to the priory*

Enter Æmilia, the Lady Abbess

ABBESS

Be quiet, people. Wherefore throng you hither?

ADRIANA

To fetch my poor distracted husband hence.
Let us come in, that we may bind him fast   40
And bear him home for his recovery.

ANGELO

I knew he was not in his perfect wits.

SECOND MERCHANT

I am sorry now that I did draw on him.

ABBESS

How long hath this possession held the man?

ADRIANA

This week he hath been heavy, sour, sad,
And much, much different from the man he was.
But till this afternoon his passion
Ne'er brake into extremity of rage.

ABBESS

Hath he not lost much wealth by wrack of sea?
Buried some dear friend? Hath not else his eye   50
Strayed his affection in unlawful love,
A sin prevailing much in youthful men,
Who give their eyes the liberty of gazing?
Which of these sorrows is he subject to?

ADRIANA

To none of these except it be the last,
Namely some love that drew him oft from home.

ABBESS

You should for that have reprehended him.

ADRIANA

Why, so I did.

ABBESS   Ay, but not rough enough.

ADRIANA
As roughly as my modesty would let me.

ABBESS

60 Haply in private.

ADRIANA   And in assemblies, too.

ABBESS
Ay, but not enough.

ADRIANA
It was the copy of our conference.
In bed he slept not for my urging it.
At board he fed not for my urging it.
Alone, it was the subject of my theme;
In company I often glanced at it.
Still did I tell him it was vile and bad.

ABBESS
And thereof came it that the man was mad.
The venom clamours of a jealous woman

70 Poisons more deadly than a mad dog's tooth.
It seems his sleeps were hindered by thy railing,
And thereof comes it that his head is light.
Thou sayst his meat was sauced with thy upbraidings.
Unquiet meals make ill digestions.
Thereof the raging fire of fever bred;
And what's a fever but a fit of madness?
Thou sayst his sports were hindered by thy brawls.
Sweet recreation barred, what doth ensue
But moody and dull melancholy,

80 Kinsman to grim and comfortless despair,
And at her heels a huge infectious troop
Of pale distemperatures and foes to life?
In food, in sport, and life-preserving rest
To be disturbed would mad or man or beast.
The consequence is, then, thy jealous fits
Hath scared thy husband from the use of wits.

LUCIANA

   She never reprehended him but mildly,
   When he demeaned himself rough, rude, and wildly.
   (*To Adriana*)
   Why bear you these rebukes, and answer not?

ADRIANA

   She did betray me to my own reproof.   90
   Good people, enter, and lay hold on him.

ABBESS

   No, not a creature enters in my house.

ADRIANA

   Then let your servants bring my husband forth.

ABBESS

   Neither. He took this place for sanctuary,
   And it shall privilege him from your hands
   Till I have brought him to his wits again,
   Or lose my labour in assaying it.

ADRIANA

   I will attend my husband, be his nurse,
   Diet his sickness, for it is my office,
   And will have no attorney but myself.   100
   And therefore let me have him home with me.

ABBESS

   Be patient, for I will not let him stir
   Till I have used the approvèd means I have,
   With wholesome syrups, drugs, and holy prayers,
   To make of him a formal man again.
   It is a branch and parcel of mine oath,
   A charitable duty of my order.
   Therefore depart, and leave him here with me.

ADRIANA

   I will not hence and leave my husband here.
   And ill it doth beseem your holiness   110
   To separate the husband and the wife.

ABBESS

Be quiet, and depart. Thou shalt not have him.   *Exit*

LUCIANA (*to Adriana*)

Complain unto the Duke of this indignity.

ADRIANA

Come, go. I will fall prostrate at his feet,
And never rise until my tears and prayers
Have won his grace to come in person hither
And take perforce my husband from the Abbess.

SECOND MERCHANT

By this, I think, the dial points at five.
Anon, I'm sure, the Duke himself in person
120 Comes this way to the melancholy vale,
The place of death and sorry execution
Behind the ditches of the abbey here.

ANGELO

Upon what cause?

SECOND MERCHANT

To see a reverend Syracusian merchant,
Who put unluckily into this bay
Against the laws and statutes of this town,
Beheaded publicly for his offence.

ANGELO

See where they come. We will behold his death.

LUCIANA

Kneel to the Duke before he pass the abbey.

> *Enter Solinus, Duke of Ephesus, and Egeon, the*
> *merchant of Syracuse, barehead, with the Headsman*
> *and other officers*

DUKE

130 Yet once again proclaim it publicly,
If any friend will pay the sum for him,
He shall not die, so much we tender him.

ADRIANA

Justice, most sacred Duke, against the Abbess!

DUKE

She is a virtuous and a reverend lady.
It cannot be that she hath done thee wrong.

ADRIANA

May it please your grace, Antipholus my husband,
Who I made lord of me and all I had
At your important letters, this ill day
A most outrageous fit of madness took him,
That desperately he hurried through the street,   140
With him his bondman all as mad as he,
Doing displeasure to the citizens
By rushing in their houses, bearing thence
Rings, jewels, anything his rage did like.
Once did I get him bound, and sent him home
Whilst to take order for the wrongs I went,
That here and there his fury had committed.
Anon, I wot not by what strong escape,
He broke from those that had the guard of him,
And with his mad attendant and himself,   150
Each one with ireful passion, with drawn swords
Met us again, and, madly bent on us,
Chased us away; till, raising of more aid,
We came again to bind them. Then they fled
Into this abbey, whither we pursued them,
And here the Abbess shuts the gates on us,
And will not suffer us to fetch him out,
Nor send him forth that we may bear him hence.
Therefore, most gracious Duke, with thy command
Let him be brought forth, and borne hence for help.   160

DUKE

Long since, thy husband served me in my wars;
And I to thee engaged a prince's word,

When thou didst make him master of thy bed,
To do him all the grace and good I could.
Go, some of you, knock at the abbey gate,
And bid the Lady Abbess come to me.
I will determine this before I stir.

Enter a Messenger

MESSENGER

O mistress, mistress, shift and save yourself!
My master and his man are both broke loose,
170   Beaten the maids a-row, and bound the Doctor,
Whose beard they have singed off with brands of fire,
And ever as it blazed they threw on him
Great pails of puddled mire to quench the hair.
My master preaches patience to him, and the while
His man with scissors nicks him like a fool.
And sure, unless you send some present help,
Between them they will kill the conjuror.

ADRIANA

Peace, fool; thy master and his man are here,
And that is false thou dost report to us.

MESSENGER

180   Mistress, upon my life I tell you true.
I have not breathed almost since I did see it.
He cries for you, and vows, if he can take you,
To scorch your face and to disfigure you.

Cry within

Hark, hark, I hear him, mistress. Fly, be gone!

DUKE

Come, stand by me. Fear nothing. Guard with halberds!

ADRIANA

Ay me, it is my husband. Witness you
That he is borne about invisible.
Even now we housed him in the abbey here,
And now he's there, past thought of human reason.

Enter Antipholus of Ephesus and Dromio of Ephesus

ANTIPHOLUS OF EPHESUS

  Justice, most gracious Duke, O grant me justice,   190
  Even for the service that long since I did thee
  When I bestrid thee in the wars, and took
  Deep scars to save thy life. Even for the blood
  That then I lost for thee, now grant me justice!

EGEON *(aside)*

  Unless the fear of death doth make me dote,
  I see my son Antipholus, and Dromio.

ANTIPHOLUS OF EPHESUS

  Justice, sweet prince, against that woman there,
  She whom thou gavest to me to be my wife;
  That hath abusèd and dishonoured me
  Even in the strength and height of injury.   200
  Beyond imagination is the wrong
  That she this day hath shameless thrown on me.

DUKE

  Discover how, and thou shalt find me just.

ANTIPHOLUS OF EPHESUS

  This day, great Duke, she shut the doors upon me
  While she with harlots feasted in my house.

DUKE

  A grievous fault. Say, woman, didst thou so?

ADRIANA

  No, my good lord. Myself, he, and my sister
  Today did dine together. So befall my soul
  As this is false he burdens me withal.

LUCIANA

  Ne'er may I look on day nor sleep on night   210
  But she tells to your highness simple truth.

ANGELO *(aside)*

  O perjured woman! They are both forsworn.
  In this the madman justly chargeth them.

ANTIPHOLUS OF EPHESUS

My liege, I am advisèd what I say,
Neither disturbed with the effect of wine
Nor heady-rash provoked with raging ire,
Albeit my wrongs might make one wiser mad.
This woman locked me out this day from dinner.
That goldsmith there, were he not packed with her,
Could witness it, for he was with me then,
Who parted with me to go fetch a chain,
Promising to bring it to the Porpentine,
Where Balthasar and I did dine together.
Our dinner done, and he not coming thither,
I went to seek him. In the street I met him,
And in his company that gentleman.
There did this perjured goldsmith swear me down
That I this day of him received the chain,
Which, God he knows, I saw not. For the which
He did arrest me with an officer.
I did obey, and sent my peasant home
For certain ducats. He with none returned.
Then fairly I bespoke the officer
To go in person with me to my house.
By the way we met
My wife, her sister, and a rabble more
Of vile confederates. Along with them
They brought one Pinch, a hungry, lean-faced villain,
A mere anatomy, a mountebank,
A threadbare juggler and a fortune-teller,
A needy, hollow-eyed, sharp-looking wretch,
A living dead man. This pernicious slave,
Forsooth, took on him as a conjuror,
And gazing in mine eyes, feeling my pulse
And with no face, as 'twere, outfacing me,
Cries out I was possessed. Then all together

They fell upon me, bound me, bore me thence,
And in a dark and dankish vault at home
There left me and my man, both bound together,
Till, gnawing with my teeth my bonds in sunder,   250
I gained my freedom, and immediately
Ran hither to your grace, whom I beseech
To give me ample satisfaction
For these deep shames and great indignities.

ANGELO
My lord, in truth, thus far I witness with him:
That he dined not at home, but was locked out.

DUKE
But had he such a chain of thee, or no?

ANGELO
He had, my lord, and when he ran in here
These people saw the chain about his neck.

SECOND MERCHANT (*to Antipholus of Ephesus*)
Besides, I will be sworn these ears of mine   260
Heard you confess you had the chain of him
After you first forswore it on the mart,
And thereupon I drew my sword on you;
And then you fled into this abbey here,
From whence I think you are come by miracle.

ANTIPHOLUS OF EPHESUS
I never came within these abbey walls,
Nor ever didst thou draw thy sword on me.
I never saw the chain, so help me heaven,
And this is false you burden me withal.

DUKE
Why, what an intricate impeach is this!   270
I think you all have drunk of Circe's cup.
If here you housed him, here he would have been.
If he were mad, he would not plead so coldly.
(*To Adriana*)

You say he dined at home. The goldsmith here
Denies that saying. (*To Dromio of Ephesus*) Sirrah, what
   say you?

DROMIO OF EPHESUS

Sir, he dined with her there at the Porpentine.

COURTESAN

He did, and from my finger snatched that ring.

ANTIPHOLUS OF EPHESUS

'Tis true, my liege, this ring I had of her.

DUKE

Sawest thou him enter at the abbey here?

COURTESAN

280   As sure, my liege, as I do see your grace.

DUKE

Why, this is strange. Go call the Abbess hither.
I think you are all mated, or stark mad.

Exit one to the Abbess

EGEON

Most mighty Duke, vouchsafe me speak a word.
Haply I see a friend will save my life
And pay the sum that may deliver me.

DUKE

Speak freely, Syracusian, what thou wilt.

EGEON

Is not your name, sir, called Antipholus?
And is not that your bondman Dromio?

DROMIO OF EPHESUS

Within this hour I was his bondman, sir,
290   But he, I thank him, gnawed in two my cords.
Now am I Dromio, and his man, unbound.

EGEON

I am sure you both of you remember me.

DROMIO OF EPHESUS

Ourselves we do remember, sir, by you,

For lately we were bound as you are now.
You are not Pinch's patient, are you, sir?

EGEON

Why look you strange on me? You know me well.

ANTIPHOLUS OF EPHESUS

I never saw you in my life till now.

EGEON

O, grief hath changed me since you saw me last,
And careful hours with time's deformèd hand
Have written strange defeatures in my face.   300
But tell me yet, dost thou not know my voice?

ANTIPHOLUS OF EPHESUS

Neither.

EGEON

Dromio, nor thou?

DROMIO OF EPHESUS

No, trust me, sir, nor I.

EGEON   I am sure thou dost?

DROMIO OF EPHESUS Ay, sir, but I am sure I do not,
   and whatsoever a man denies you are now bound to
   believe him.

EGEON

Not know my voice? O time's extremity,
Hast thou so cracked and splitted my poor tongue
In seven short years that here my only son   310
Knows not my feeble key of untuned cares?
Though now this grainèd face of mine be hid
In sap-consuming winter's drizzled snow,
And all the conduits of my blood froze up,
Yet hath my night of life some memory,
My wasting lamps some fading glimmer left,
My dull deaf ears a little use to hear.
All these old witnesses, I cannot err,
Tell me thou art my son Antipholus.

ANTIPHOLUS OF EPHESUS

320 I never saw my father in my life.

EGEON

But seven years since, in Syracusa, boy,
Thou knowest we parted. But perhaps, my son,
Thou shamest to acknowledge me in misery.

ANTIPHOLUS OF EPHESUS

The Duke and all that know me in the city
Can witness with me that it is not so.
I ne'er saw Syracusa in my life.

DUKE

I tell thee, Syracusian, twenty years
Have I been patron to Antipholus,
During which time he ne'er saw Syracusa.

330 I see thy age and dangers make thee dote.

Enter Æmilia, the Abbess, with Antipholus of
Syracuse and Dromio of Syracuse

ABBESS

Most mighty Duke, behold a man much wronged.

All gather to see them

ADRIANA

I see two husbands, or mine eyes deceive me.

DUKE

One of these men is *genius* to the other;
And so, of these, which is the natural man,
And which the spirit? Who deciphers them?

DROMIO OF SYRACUSE

I, sir, am Dromio. Command him away.

DROMIO OF EPHESUS

I, sir, am Dromio. Pray let me stay.

ANTIPHOLUS OF SYRACUSE

Egeon art thou not? or else his ghost.

DROMIO OF SYRACUSE

O, my old master – who hath bound him here?

ABBESS

Whoever bound him, I will loose his bonds,   340
And gain a husband by his liberty.
Speak, old Egeon, if thou beest the man
That hadst a wife once called Æmilia,
That bore thee at a burden two fair sons.
O, if thou beest the same Egeon, speak,
And speak unto the same Æmilia.

DUKE

Why, here begins his morning story right.
These two Antipholus', these two so like,
And these two Dromios, one in semblance,
Besides her urging of her wrack at sea –   350
These are the parents to these children,
Which accidentally are met together.

EGEON

If I dream not, thou art Æmilia.
If thou art she, tell me, where is that son
That floated with thee on the fatal raft?

ABBESS

By men of Epidamnum he and I
And the twin Dromio all were taken up.
But by and by rude fishermen of Corinth
By force took Dromio and my son from them,
And me they left with those of Epidamnum.   360
What then became of them I cannot tell.
I, to this fortune that you see me in.

DUKE (*to Antipholus of Syracuse*)

Antipholus, thou camest from Corinth first.

ANTIPHOLUS OF SYRACUSE

No, sir, not I. I came from Syracuse.

DUKE

Stay, stand apart. I know not which is which.

ANTIPHOLUS OF EPHESUS
I came from Corinth, my most gracious lord.
DROMIO OF EPHESUS
And I with him.
ANTIPHOLUS OF EPHESUS
Brought to this town by that most famous warrior
Duke Menaphon, your most renownèd uncle.
ADRIANA
370 Which of you two did dine with me today?
ANTIPHOLUS OF SYRACUSE
I, gentle mistress.
ADRIANA   And are not you my husband?
ANTIPHOLUS OF EPHESUS
No, I say nay to that.
ANTIPHOLUS OF SYRACUSE
And so do I. Yet did she call me so,
And this fair gentlewoman, her sister here,
Did call me brother. (*To Luciana*) What I told you then
I hope I shall have leisure to make good,
If this be not a dream I see and hear.
ANGELO
That is the chain, sir, which you had of me.
ANTIPHOLUS OF SYRACUSE
I think it be, sir. I deny it not.
ANTIPHOLUS OF EPHESUS
380 And you, sir, for this chain arrested me.
ANGELO
I think I did, sir. I deny it not.
ADRIANA (*to Antipholus of Ephesus*)
I sent you money, sir, to be your bail
By Dromio, but I think he brought it not.
DROMIO OF EPHESUS
No, none by me.

ANTIPHOLUS OF SYRACUSE

This purse of ducats I received from you,
And Dromio my man did bring them me.
I see we still did meet each other's man,
And I was ta'en for him, and he for me,
And thereupon these errors are arose.

ANTIPHOLUS OF EPHESUS

These ducats pawn I for my father here.   390

DUKE

It shall not need. Thy father hath his life.

COURTESAN

Sir, I must have that diamond from you.

ANTIPHOLUS OF EPHESUS

There, take it, and much thanks for my good cheer.

ABBESS

Renownèd Duke, vouchsafe to take the pains
To go with us into the abbey here,
And hear at large discoursèd all our fortunes,
And all that are assembled in this place,
That by this sympathizèd one day's error
Have suffered wrong. Go, keep us company,
And we shall make full satisfaction.   400
Thirty-three years have I but gone in travail
Of you, my sons, and till this present hour
My heavy burden ne'er deliverèd.
The Duke, my husband, and my children both,
And you, the calendars of their nativity,
Go to a gossips' feast, and go with me.
After so long grief, such nativity.

DUKE

With all my heart I'll gossip at this feast.

*Exeunt all but the two Dromios and the
two brothers Antipholus*

DROMIO OF SYRACUSE (*to Antipholus of Ephesus*)
  Master, shall I fetch your stuff from shipboard?

ANTIPHOLUS OF EPHESUS

410 Dromio, what stuff of mine hast thou embarked?

DROMIO OF SYRACUSE
  Your goods that lay at host, sir, in the Centaur.

ANTIPHOLUS OF SYRACUSE
  He speaks to me – I am your master, Dromio!
  Come, go with us, we'll look to that anon.
  Embrace thy brother there, rejoice with him.

Exeunt the brothers Antipholus

DROMIO OF SYRACUSE
  There is a fat friend at your master's house
  That kitchened me for you today at dinner.
  She now shall be my sister, not my wife!

DROMIO OF EPHESUS
  Methinks you are my glass, and not my brother.
  I see by you I am a sweet-faced youth.

420 Will you walk in to see their gossiping?

DROMIO OF SYRACUSE
  Not I, sir. You are my elder.

DROMIO OF EPHESUS
  That's a question. How shall we try it?

DROMIO OF SYRACUSE
  We'll draw cuts for the senior. Till then, lead thou first.

DROMIO OF EPHESUS
  Nay then, thus:
  We came into the world like brother and brother,
  And now let's go hand in hand, not one before another.

Exeunt

COMMENTARY

'F' here refers to the first Folio, 1623 (see 'An Account of the Text', pages 183–4). Biblical quotations are modernized from the Bishops' Bible (1568 etc.), the version likely to have been best known to Shakespeare. Quotations from Warner's translation of *Menaechmi* are modernized from the reprint in *Narrative and Dramatic Sources of Shakespeare*, edited by Geoffrey Bullough, Volume I (1957).

(stage direction) *Solinus* (pronounced to rhyme with 'minus'). The Duke's name is not mentioned elsewhere in the play. Caius Julius Solinus, who lived probably in the third century A.D., wrote *Polyhistor*, which was published in an English translation by Arthur Golding in 1587 as *The Excellent and Pleasant Works of Julius Solinus Polyhistor*. Shakespeare may have looked at it in connexion with the geography of the play. But he could have known Solinus's name without knowing his book; and there is a character of the same name in John Lyly's play *Campaspe*, printed in 1584.

Ephesus. Historically, Ephesus was an Ionian, Syracuse a Doric city, so enmity between them would have been natural enough. Plautus's setting is Epidamnus. The change may have been influenced by the relationship between Shakespeare's thematic interests in the play and the content of St Paul's Epistle to the Ephesians (see Introduction, pages 28–9), and by Ephesus's reputation as a place of sorcery and magic. It is to Ephesus that the chest containing the apparently dead body of Apollonius's wife, Lucina, floats in Gower's *Confessio Amantis*, the source of Shakespeare's framework story.

Egeon (so spelt in F; sometimes partially classicized to 'Aegeon'; pronounced to rhyme with 'Fijian')

Syracuse (the chief town of Sicily. F uses spellings ending in 'e', 'a', and 'ia' indiscriminately except that scansion sometimes demands the strong ending, as in line 3 below.)

1 *Proceed* (probably 'set in action (or "continue") the legal proceedings . . .' rather than 'move forward . . .'. This is a trial scene.)

2 *doom* sentence

3 *Syracusa*. The first syllable is long, as in 'sire'.

plead no more. Egeon seems to have been embracing his fate rather than pleading against it; but perhaps his *end woes and all* is interpreted as a plea for sympathy.

4 *partial to* biased so as to. (*Partial* here is the opposite of 'impartial'.)

6 *outrage* violence

7 *well-dealing* (probably used in the general sense of 'conducting themselves well' rather than specifically 'conducting their business well')

8 *wanting* lacking

guilders. The *guilder* was a Dutch and German silver coin which seems to have had some currency in Elizabethan England. Shakespeare uses it here and at IV.1.4 in a general sense of 'money'. It does not occur elsewhere in his work.

redeem ransom

9 *sealed . . . with their bloods* (alluding to the red sealing-wax used on legal documents)

10 *Excludes*. The singular form of the verb with a plural subject was acceptable Elizabethan grammar.

11 *intestine* (synonymous with *mortal*; but also 'internal' in that Syracuse and Ephesus were both Greek city-states)

jars conflicts

12 *seditious* turbulent

13 *synods* legislative assemblies

15 *admit no traffic to our adverse towns* permit no trade
between our hostile towns

16–18 *Nay . . . fairs.* F reads:

> Nay more, if any borne at *Ephesus*
> Be seene at any *Siracusian* Marts and Fayres:

Most editors retain the division into two lines, omit-
ting 'any' before '*Siracusian*' on the assumption that
it is an accidental intrusion, since the word occurs also
in the previous and the following lines. This may be so.
But it is also possible that 'Nay more' should be
regarded as a line on its own. Ejaculations are frequently extra-metrical.

18 *marts* markets

21 *confiscate* (past participle; accented on the second
syllable) forfeited
dispose disposal

22 *marks.* A *mark* was not a coin but a unit of 13s. 4d.
levièd raised

23 *quit* pay

24 *substance* property, wealth

27–8 *Yet this my comfort: when your words are done,* | *My
woes end likewise with the evening sun.* The exact meaning of this couplet is not clear. Perhaps it means 'Yet
this is my comfort: that just as your speech will come to
an end, so, when the sun sets, will my misfortunes'; or
'Yet, now that you have finished speaking, this is my
comfort: my misfortunes . . .'; or perhaps 'Yet let this
be my comfort when you have finished speaking: that
when evening comes my misfortunes, too, will cease.'

27 *this.* Shakespeare often omits 'is', here perhaps to
avoid an ugly sound.

28 *evening sun.* Shakespeare begins the series of references
that define the play's time-span.

35 *by nature* as the result of natural affection (which causes him to seek his son)

36 *what my sorrow gives me leave* (that is, 'as much as I can say without breaking down')

38–9 *happy but for me, | And by me, had not our hap been bad* happy except in me; and who would have been happy in me, too, had we not had a misfortune

39 *And by me, had not our hap been bad.* The line is short. Editors sometimes follow the unauthoritative second Folio (1632) in adding 'too' after *me*, but this is unnecessary. The pause is dramatically effective.

 hap fortune

40 *increased* (probably the participle – 'being increased . . .' – rather than the active verb)

42 *Epidamnum.* F has '*Epidamium*' throughout. This seems to be a misreading of *Epidamnum*, which is the name of the city in Warner's *Menaechmi*, though its real name was Epidamnus. It was on the coast of Illyricum on the Adriatic Sea. The action of *Menaechmi* takes place there, not in Ephesus.

 factor agent

43 *care of* anxiety about

 at random untended (as a result of the factor's death)

44 *kind* loving

53 *could not be distinguished but by names.* The implication is that Egeon was intelligent enough to give them different names, though this is not actually stated and would of course have been destructive of the ensuing action. See Commentary to line 129, and to I.2 (stage direction), *of Syracuse*.

55 *mean woman.* The line is short, and is sometimes regularized by reading 'meaner woman' or 'poor, mean woman'. It is possible that 'mean' was pronounced as two syllables.

 mean poor, lowly

56 *burden male.* The phrase is not recorded, though 'child male', 'heir male', etc. are used in legal terminology.

The punctuation is often emended to make *male* qualify *twins*.

58 *bought*. Slaves appear frequently in Plautus's adaptations of Greek plays, often enjoying a privileged position in the household.

59 *not meanly* not a little

60 *motions* requests, entreaties, proposals

62 *We came aboard*. These words are printed as part of the preceding line in F. Some editors think they were part of a line of which the remainder has been lost. But short lines are not uncommon in Shakespeare, especially in long speeches. This one may mark Egeon's emotion, but is also probably part of the direct imitation of incomplete lines in heroic narrative in Virgil.

63 *league* (about three miles. In English the word has had only literary use.)

65 *tragic instance* omen, ominous sign

68 *fearful* frightened

69 *doubtful* dreadful (conveying fear, not doubt)
   warrant of authorization for (part of the legal metaphor present also in *grant* and *convey*)

73 *plainings* plaints, wailings

74 *for fashion* (because the others did)

75 *delays* (from death)

76 *this* thus. Two interpretations are possible, and can be suggested by the punctuation: 'Thus it came about that the sailors . . .', and 'This is how it happened: . . .'. The former is preferred here because it attributes a more continuous flow to the narrative.

77 *our boat* (the ship's boat – in which the sailors might have been expected to find room for their passengers)

79 *careful for* concerned about
   the latter-born the younger (but see line 125 and Commentary)

80–81 *spare mast | Such as seafaring men provide for storms*. This is a reference to the use in an emergency of a

123

'yard' – a spar normally fitted to a mast to support a sail – as a mast, when it was known as a jury-mast.

83   *like* similarly, equally

85   *on whom* on him on whom

87   *straight* immediately

stream current. There may be an allusion to the strong current referred to in *Othello*, III.3.450–53:

> the Pontic Sea,
> Whose icy current and compulsive course
> Ne'er feels retiring ebb, but keeps due on
> To the Propontic and the Hellespont.

88   *Was*. The syntax is not unusual by Elizabethan standards.

Corinth. See Commentary to line 94.

90   *vapours* clouds

offended assailed

91   *benefit* benefaction

93   *amain* quickly, at full speed

94   *Of Corinth that, of Epidaurus this*. The line seems to imply that the ships were coming from opposite directions, which is not possible, as both Corinth and Epidaurus were south-east of Epidamnum. But there was another Epidaurus (now Dubrovnik), north of Epidamnum. Shakespeare may have been confused by this. Geography was not his strongest suit. To read 'Epidamnum' here (meaning that the ship was coming from the town where Egeon and his family had embarked) would be tidier, since at V.1.356 the Abbess says that she was picked up *By men of Epidamnum*; but the inconsistency would be unlikely to trouble an audience. The line could presumably also mean simply that one ship was, as it were, registered at each town. *Corinth*. The name may have been suggested to Shakespeare by Acts 19.1: 'while Apollos was at Corinth, Paul passed through the upper coasts, and came to Ephesus'.

96   *that* that which

100   *Worthily* justly

101   *meet* (presumably 'meet us' rather than 'meet each other')

       leagues. When the word had any precision of meaning it was about three miles (see Commentary to line 63), but this seems too much here. A general impression of considerable distance is all that is intended.

104   *ship* (the mast)

107   *What* something

109   *With lesser weight* (because it carried the woman and her younger child)

112   *as we thought.* At this point, Egeon does not know for certain that he was wrong; but admission of doubt prepares the audience for the fact that he was.

114   *hap* chance

116   *reft* bereft, robbed forcefully

123   *dilate* relate, describe

124   *What have befallen of* what (things) have happened to

125   *My youngest boy.* The inconsistency with line 79 is probably a mere accident.

126–7 *inquisitive | After* eager for information about

127   *importuned.* The accent is on the second syllable.

128   *so his case was like* so alike was his case

129   *Reft of his brother, but retained his name.* The construction is odd; *retained* perhaps is equivalent to 'having retained'. The idea is that each twin who has remained with Egeon has the same name as his brother – the seeds of the ensuing confusion are being set. See Commentary to line 53.

131–2 *Whom whilst I laboured of a love to see, | I hazarded the loss of whom I loved* for so long as I strove through love to see him, I risked the loss of the other whom also I loved

133–5 *Five summers … Ephesus.* Shakespeare seems here to be adapting *Menaechmi*, where (in Warner's translation) Messenio says: 'six years now have we roamed about thus, Istria, Hispania, Massilia, Illyria, all the upper sea, all High Greece, all haven towns in Italy ...' (edited by Bullough, page 17). By 'High Greece' Shakespeare seems to have understood the Greek cities of Asia Minor and the Levant, though in the original it refers to an area of Southern Italy known as *Magna Graecia*.

135   *coasting* travelling along the coast (from port to port)

136   *Hopeless* despairing
         unsought unsearched

137   *Or* either

140   *travels* (combining the modern sense with 'travails' – 'labours', 'efforts')

141   *Hapless* luckless

145   *would they* (even) if they would
         disannul abolish, cancel

149   *But* except
         disparagement disgrace, injury

151   *limit* appoint

152   *To seek thy health by beneficial help* (a disputed line; see Emendations, page 185, and Rejected Emendations, page 187.)
         health salvation

156   *Gaoler, take him to thy custody.* This short line has sometimes been expanded, for example to 'Gaoler, go take ...', but it seems appropriate to the change in tone and address.

159   *procrastinate* postpone

I.2   (stage direction) *Antipholus.* The name is related to the Greek *antiphilos*, 'mutual affection'. Shakespeare may have remembered the Antiphilus of Sidney's *Arcadia* (Book 2), who is loved by Erona and rescued by her from prison, but loves another. When he becomes king he justifies polygamy, and is killed by women.
    of Syracuse. F has '*Erotes*', and in the stage direction

at II.1.0 calls the other brother '*Antipholis Sereptus*'. This method of distinguishing the brothers is not employed in the dialogue, and its significance is unclear. *Erotes* may be related to the Latin verb *errare*, 'to wander'; or perhaps it refers to 'Erotium', the name of the Courtesan in *Menaechmi*, since it is this Antipholus who receives her favours. *Sereptus* is more clearly a form of *surreptus*, 'stolen away'. The word is several times used by Plautus of the brother who was taken away in infancy, and in Shakespeare's time the character was referred to as 'Menaechmus Subreptus'. Shakespeare may have toyed with, but rejected, the idea of distinguishing the brothers by names (see I.1.53).

First Merchant. In F there is nothing to distinguish him from the Merchant who first appears in IV.1 and is clearly a different character.

Dromio. There is a servant of this name in John Lyly's play *Mother Bombie*, printed in 1594 but probably written and performed some years previously. But it derives from 'Dromo', the name given to a slave in several of Terence's comedies.

2   *Lest that* lest. (*That*, as in other, similar, constructions, merely adds emphasis.)

    too very

9   *the Centaur* (an inn)

    host lodge

11   *dinner-time* (between eleven and twelve. See line 45.)

13   *Peruse* survey

18   *mean* opportunity (and also perhaps the 'means' or wealth which he is carrying)

19   *villain* (used playfully) bondman

20   *dull with care and melancholy*. Antipholus of Syracuse is presented as more introspective and liable to melancholy than his brother. It is perhaps significant that this Antipholus soliloquizes whereas the other does not.

21   *humour* mood, disposition (with perhaps a more physical connotation in Shakespeare's time, when *melancholy* was believed to be a dark and heavy substance, or *humour*, in the veins, in need of 'lightening') *his merry jests*. This prepares us for Antipholus's assumption that his servant is joking when the twin Dromio enters at line 40.

25   *benefit* profit

26   *Soon at*. The phrase seems to have had various meanings including 'towards' and 'about'; and 'soon' alone could mean 'in the early evening'. 'Soon at' seems also to have been used in an approximation to the modern sense, implying that the time, when it comes, will be welcome. It is not possible to determine which sense is uppermost here.

       five o'clock. This is gradually established as the hour at which the action will be resolved. See III.2.182, where Angelo says he will collect payment for his chain at *supper-time*, IV.1.10, where he says he will do so at *five o'clock* (a common hour for supper), and V.1.118 (*By this, I think, the dial points at five*), where five o'clock is seen as the limit of the time that the Duke has appointed for Egeon to raise the money for his ransom (I.1.151).

27   *Please you* if it pleases you, if you agree

28   *consort* attend, accompany

29   *present* pressing, urgent

30   *lose myself* roam around. But in conjunction with line 40, and the later events of the play, the literal meaning has a special irony.

32   *commend you to your own content* wish you all you wish yourself

35   *to the world* in relation to the world (as the drop of water is in relation to the ocean)

       a drop of water. The image is picked up again by Adriana at II.2.135. (See Introduction, page 29.) It comes appropriately after Egeon's account of his family's adventures at sea and his sea-wanderings in search of his sons. It parallels *Menaechmi*, II.1, where Messenio, the slave, says to the seeking Antipholus 'I think if we had sought a needle all this time, we must needs have found it, had it been above ground' and 'This is washing of a blackamoor' (edited by Bullough, page 17).

37   *Who* which
     find his fellow forth seek its counterpart out

38   *Unseen* ('lacking skill or experience', or perhaps 'indistinguishable')
     inquisitive seeking knowledge
     confounds himself destroys its own identity

39   *to find a mother and a brother.* This helps the audience to identify Antipholus as Egeon's son.

40   *In quest of them unhappy* unlucky in the search for them. Most editors read 'In quest of them, unhappy, ...'.
     lose myself. The phrase is echoed from line 30, but now has much deeper significance. Harold Brooks comments: 'The theme of identity is here linked with those of relationship (dislocated or re-established), and of risk. To seek reunion with the lost members of the family, Antipholus is risking his identity; yet he must do so, for only if the full relationship is restored can he find content. And then, hints the image of one water-drop seeking another, the present individual identity will be lost, or transformed, in another way.... Antipholus' fear that he is losing himself is full of comic irony. No sooner has he expressed it, than, with the entry of his brother's Dromio, he begins to be the victim of the successive mistakes of identity to which his words are designed by Shakespeare as a prelude, and in the course of which he will come to wonder whether he is beside himself, and has lost himself indeed' ('Themes and Structure in *The Comedy of Errors*', pages 58–9).

41   *almanac of my true date* (Dromio, who was born at the same hour as his master, and is thus an *almanac* or calendar by which Antipholus can determine his *date*, or age. In the circumstances, the description is ironical.)

42   *How chance* how does it happen that

43–52   Dromio's energetic style brings a new tone into
etc.   the play, marking the assault of the unexpected upon Antipholus's consciousness. See Introduction, page 21.

43   *Returned ... approached.* Dromio is coming rather than coming back.

45   *twelve.* The usual Elizabethan dinner-time was between eleven and twelve.

47   *hot* angry

49   *stomach* appetite

51   *fast and pray* (as penance)

52   *penitent* undergoing penance; (specifically) fasting; sorry
       default fault, offence

53   *Stop in your wind* hold your breath (tongue); shut up

55   *O.* Dromio has to think what money is referred to.
       o' on

56   *crupper* (a leather strap securing a horse's saddle)

58   *humour* mood

61   *charge* responsibility (that with which he has been charged)

63   *in post* in haste

64   *post* (used like a door-post on which tavern-reckonings were scored; beaten)

65   *scour* beat (with a pun on 'score')

66   *maw* belly
       clock. F reads 'cooke', which could be defended; but emendation to *clock* is supported by *strike* in the following line. There was a proverbial expression, 'The belly is the truest clock.'

72   *have done* make an end of

73–4   *thy charge ... My charge* the money with which you were entrusted ... the task I was given

75   *the Phoenix* (Antipholus's house, also apparently his shop, identified by the sign of a phoenix)

76   *stays* (the singular form of the verb with a plural subject, as commonly) wait

77   *as I am a Christian* (a common saying)

79   *sconce* head

80   *stands* on insists on playing
     undisposed not in the mood

81   *thousand marks.* Though Antipholus does not know it, this is the sum needed to ransom his father (I.1.22).

85   *pay . . . again* pay back (with a pun on *pay* meaning 'beat')

90   *prays* (leading on from *fast* in the previous line; compare line 51)
     hie you hasten

94   *an* (regularly spelt 'and' in F and some modern editions) if
     take my heels take to my heels, run away. (The expression is used especially for contrast with *hold your hands*.)

95   *device* trick

96   *o'er-raught* over-reached, cheated

97-102 *They say . . . liberties of sin.* This derives mainly from *Menaechmi*, where, at the beginning of Act II, Messenio says: 'this town Epidamnum is a place of outrageous expenses, exceeding in all riot and lasciviousness, and, I hear, as full of ribalds, parasites, drunkards, catchpoles, coney-catchers, and sycophants as it can hold. Then for courtesans, why, here's the currentest stamp of them in the world' (edited by Bullough, page 17). Shakespeare deliberately lays emphasis on magic (see Introduction, page 31). The passage may also owe something to Acts 19, where inhabitants of Ephesus who used 'curious arts' are mentioned, and to the town's general notoriety for magical practices.

97   *cozenage* cheating

98   *As* such as
101   *mountebanks* itinerant quacks, salesmen
102   *liberties* unrestrained acts

II.1   (stage direction) *Adriana.* The vowels are pronounced
        as in 'made it rather' or 'made it later'.
        Luciana. The first two syllables are pronounced as in
        'Lucy'; the name may rhyme with 'garner' or 'saner'.

3   *two o'clock.* It was at least twelve o'clock in the
        previous scene: I.2.45.

7–9   *A man is master of his liberty.* | *Time is their master,*
        and when they see time | *They'll go or come.* The
        sequence of thought is not clear. Luciana seems at
        first to say that men can command their own time,
        and then to take the opposite point of view again.
        Perhaps she means 'So far as we are concerned,
        men will do as they please; but they are nevertheless
        subject to the demands of time, and will come or go
        as their larger responsibilities permit.'

7   *A man is master of his liberty.* This sounds proverbial,
        but is not recorded.

8   *see time* see fit

9   *If so* (if what I have said is true; this being so)
        patient. See Introduction, pages 26–8.

10–43   Couplets mark the formality of the disputation on
        marriage.

10–11   *liberty . . . out o'door.* There is some word-play here,
        resulting from *liberty* as (1) freedom, (2) the district
        extending beyond the bounds of a city which was
        under the control of the municipal authority, and also
        the limits outside the doors of a prison in which
        prisoners were sometimes allowed to live.

11   *still* always

12   *Look when* whenever

13   *he is the bridle of your will* (perhaps related to Proverbs
        26.3: 'Unto the horse belongeth a whip, to the ass a
        bridle, and a rod to the fool's back')

132

15   *lashed* scourged, punished (as an ass is whipped).
      There may be some sense of 'lashed in', 'restrained'.
16   *heaven's eye* (the sun)
17   *his* its
      bound boundary, limit
20–25 *Man . . . accords.* Various biblical passages may have
      influenced these lines. The idea that man is master of
      the animal kingdom is stated in Psalm 8.6–8: 'Thou
      makest him to have dominion of the works of thy
      hands: and thou hast put all things in subjection
      under his feet; All sheep and oxen: yea, and the beasts
      of the field; The fowls of the air, and the fishes of the
      sea: and whatsoever walketh through the paths of the
      seas'. The word *pre-eminence* occurs in a related
      context in Ecclesiastes 3.19: 'a man hath no pre-
      eminence above a beast.' Man's dominion is also stated
      in Genesis: 'God said "Let us make man in our
      image, after our likeness, and let them have rule of
      the fish of the sea, and of the fowl of the air, and of
      cattle, and of all the earth, and of every creeping thing
      that creepeth upon the earth. . . ." And God said
      unto them "Be fruitful, and multiply, and replenish
      the earth, and subdue it, and have dominion of the
      fish of the sea, and fowl of the air, and of every living
      thing that walketh upon the earth" ' (1.26–8). And the
      idea that women should submit to men is stated in St
      Paul's Epistle to the Ephesians: 'Wives, submit
      yourselves unto your own husbands, as unto the Lord:
      For the husband is the head of the wife, even as Christ
      is the head of the Church . . . as the Church is subject
      unto Christ, likewise the wives to their own husbands
      in all things . . . let the wife reverence her husband'
      (5.22–33; paraphrased in the Homily 'Of the State of
      Matrimony'). Shakespeare makes Katherina express
      similar sentiments in the climactic speech of *The
      Taming of the Shrew* (V.2.135–78), another play much
      concerned with the marriage relationship.

20   *more divine* (nearer to God on the scale of creation)

24   *Are* (taking its subject, *Man*, in the plural sense)

25   *attend on their accords* wait on their consent

27   *troubles* (fear of troubles)

29   *obey* (in contrast to *bear some sway*: Luciana implies
      that to learn to obey is better preparation for marriage
      than to learn to rule)

30   *start some otherwhere* should move elsewhere, chase
      another woman

31   *forbear* be patient, restrain my anger

32   *Patience unmoved! No marvel though she pause.* In her
      incredulity Adriana moves into the third person,
      perhaps addressing the audience.
      No marvel though she pause no wonder she delays (to
      marry)

33   *other cause* cause to behave otherwise

39   *helpless* unavailing, useless

40   *like right bereft* the same rights (of marriage) torn
      away from you

41   *fool-begged* foolish (said to allude to a practice of
      applying for custody of a lunatic in order to gain
      control of his property; thus the word was used of a
      characteristic that brings disadvantages as well as
      profit)
      left abandoned

42   *but to try* just to put it to the proof

45   *at two hands* (alluding to Dromio's beating at I.2.92)

48   *told* communicated (with a hint of 'counted out', as
      with blows)

49   *understand* (punningly: 'stand under the force of', as
      also in line 54)

50–53 *doubtfully ... doubtfully* ambiguously ... dreadfully

57   *horn-mad* furious (as of animals ready to use their
      horns). Adriana understands him to mean 'mad
      because cuckolded'.

60–74 (This is not a strictly accurate account of what
      happened when Antipholus of Syracuse asked Dromio

of Ephesus for his gold, but rather a conflation of the happenings of I.2.43–94.)

67   *Hang up* (a mild oath – literally 'hang')

68   *Out on* (an expression of indignation)

72–3   *my errand, due unto my tongue, ... I bare home upon my shoulders* I carried back on my shoulders (as a beating) the message (*errand*) that should have been given to me to deliver by my tongue

79   *An* if. F reads 'And', as always whether the word means modern 'and' or 'if'. Editors take it in the former sense, punctuating the lines as two independent statements. The reading adopted here seems more in keeping with Dromio's resiliently ironical attitude.
     bless (1) consecrate; (2) wound, hurt
     cross (1) crossness; (2) sign of the cross

80   *holy* (punningly)

81   *peasant* (used contemptuously) servant

82   *round* (1) outspoken; (2) spherical. (This is the rhetorical figure of 'syllepsis', the use of a word having simultaneously two different meanings.)

83   *football*. The game was even rougher in Shakespeare's day than now. Sir Thomas Elyot (*The Governor*, 1531, Book I, Chapter 27) found in it 'nothing but beastly fury and extreme violence', and later King James I, perhaps under Elyot's influence, condemned 'all rough and violent exercise, as the football, meeter for laming than making able the users thereof' (*Basilicon Doron*, 1599, Book III).

83, 84   *spurn* kick

87   *do ... grace* give pleasure to
     minions darlings, mistresses

88   *starve* die

89   *homely age* age which brings plainness

90   *wasted* ('squandered' and 'worn away')

91   *discourses* conversation

92   *sharp* witty

93   *blunts it more than marble hard* blunts it more than hard

marble would. (*Sharp discourse* is imagined as a knife being blunted by the *marble* of *Unkindness*.)

94   *bait* tempt. Another possible reading is 'bate', that is 'diminish his affection for me'.

97   *ground* cause

98   *defeatures* disfigurement. The word is used again at V.1.300. Its only other occurrence in Shakespeare is in *Venus and Adonis*, line 736.

       fair (noun) beauty

100   *deer* (and 'dear')

       pale enclosure

101   *from* away from

       stale. The basic meaning is 'decoy'. The word probably had some special meaning in connexion with *deer*; Adriana implies that she is ridiculed or held in contempt in comparison with her rival.

103   *with . . . dispense* disregard, pardon

105   *lets it but he would be here* prevents (*lets*) him from being here

107   *alone a love*. This is one of the most disputed phrases in the play. F reads 'alone, a loue'. Among suggested emendations are 'alone alone', 'alone o' love', and 'alone a toy'. Presumably the general sense is either 'I would not mind if he kept that (the chain)' or 'I wish that he would keep his love to himself'. Since none of the proposed alterations seems satisfactory, F's reading is preferred here, awkward though it is, in the possibility that it is intended to mean 'Would that he kept his (other) love to himself provided that . . .'.

108   *keep fair quarter with* play fair in regard to, behave honourably concerning

109   *the jewel best enamellèd* (even) the best-enamelled gold ornament. 'Jewel' meant any ornament, not necessarily a precious stone.

110   *his* its

       still continually

110–14 F reads:

> yet the gold bides still
> That others touch, and often touching will,
> Where gold and no man that hath a name,
> By falshood and corruption doth it shame.

This is obviously corrupt. Many improvements have been suggested, none of them completely satisfactory. The frequent alteration of 'Where' to 'Wear' seems to be supported by antithesis with 'bides'. 'By' could be right if Adriana means 'No (sensible) man (willingly) shames his reputation', but emendation of 'By' to 'But' seems to produce better sense. The present edition assumes that behind these lines lies the following meaning: 'Even the best-enamelled golden ornament will tarnish. Yet the gold itself retains its value, even though people other than its owner touch it. Nevertheless, frequent "touching" will wear gold away; similarly, no man's reputation can remain untainted if he behaves in a corrupt and false manner.' In this metaphor the 'ornament' is her husband, who has lost his beauty in her eyes. She admits that he retains value for 'others', but suggests that this value, too, is liable to dwindle.

But this interpretation is in itself faulty, since the 'jewel' could be interpreted as Adriana's beauty rather than Antipholus's worth, and in line 111 the word *and* suggests 'therefore' or 'moreover' rather than 'nevertheless'. It may be that *and* is erroneous, since it comes again in the following line. The corruption of the passage is such that it is best omitted in performance.

111   *touching.* To *touch* gold is to test its quality by rubbing it on a touchstone, a process which, if continued, would rub it away.

112   *Wear gold.* I take this to mean 'wear gold away'. But a possible interpretation is 'remain gold still'. If this

were adopted, we should have to interpret *often touching will | Wear gold* as 'being often tried, or touched (perhaps with some sexual implications), gold will still remain itself'.

116   *fond* credulous

II.2   This scene opens in no specific locality, but becomes Antipholus of Ephesus's house with the entrance of Adriana and Luciana at line 118.

1–4   This refers back to I.2.9–18.

3   *in care* conscientiously

4   *By computation and mine host's report* by thinking out where I am likely to be (Dromio knows his master's plans – I.2.11–14), along with whatever the host has been able to tell him. Some editors end a sentence with *out* (line 3) and remove the stop after *report* (line 4), but this does not seem to improve the sense.

19   *feltest* (in his beating, I.2.92)

22   *flout me in the teeth* insult me to my face

24   *earnest* (punning on the senses of 'serious' and 'money paid as a deposit for a *bargain*')

27   *for* as

fool (one who stands in the familiar, friendly relationship of a fool to his master)

28   *jest upon* trifle with

29   *make a common of my serious hours* intrude on my hours of seriousness as if they were common property

30–31   *When the sun shines let foolish gnats make sport, | But creep in crannies when he hides his beams.* The lines have a sententiously proverbial sound, but are not recorded as a proverb.

32   *aspect* (accented on the second syllable. In astrology the *aspect* of a planet referred to its position, and thus to its possible influence on human behaviour. Antipholus continues the line of imagery begun with *sun*.)

34   *this method* this procedure that I have just described

sconce head (punning in the following lines on *sconce* as a small fort, subject to *battering*, and also as a screen or shelter)

35 *So* provided that

38 *ensconce* protect, conceal

38-9 *in my shoulders* (where it will have retreated). There was a proverb 'He has more in his head than you in both your shoulders.'

39 *why am I beaten?* After their altercation, master and servant revert to their usual friendly relationship in a passage of jesting largely based on proverbial expressions.

45 *every why hath a wherefore* (proverbial)

48 *out of season* unseasonably, unjustly

49 *neither rhyme nor reason* (proverbial)
rhyme measure

55 *to give you nothing for something* by giving you nothing in return for your services

57 *wants* lacks

58 *that* that which

59 *In good time* (a colloquial expression) indeed! very well!

61 *Basting* (punningly)

67 *choleric* irritable (having too much of the hot and dry humour of choler, supposed to be created by certain types of food). Compare *The Taming of the Shrew*, IV.1.156-8, where Petruchio says that the meat he was offered was

> burnt and dried away,
> And I expressly am forbid to touch it,
> For it engenders choler, planteth anger.

68 *dry* severe. (Properly a *dry* blow was one that did not break the skin or draw blood.)

69-70 *in good time* seasonably

70 *There's a time for all things* (proverbial)

74   *Marry* (originally a mild oath) why

75   *plain bald pate of Father Time himself.* Father Time was usually portrayed as bald except for a forelock.

78   *recover* (playing on 're-cover' and anticipating the legal imagery of the following lines)

79–80   *fine and recovery* (legal terminology referring to the transfer of property. The process was one by which property could be taken out of entail into full ownership.)

81   *fine* fee

82   *lost hair of another man.* Wigs were made of human hair.

84   *excrement* outgrowth (a normal use)

86   *scanted* withheld from, been niggardly of to

87   *wit* intelligence

88–9   *there's many a man hath more hair than wit* (proverbial)

90–91   *he hath the wit to lose his hair.* This is an allusion to the consequences of syphilis. Dr Johnson's note on lines 88–9 is 'That is, *those who have more hair than wit*, are easily entrapped by loose women, and suffer the consequences of lewdness, one of which, in the first appearance of the disease in Europe, was the loss of hair.'

93   *plain dealers* men without deceit. Antipholus seems to mean 'You said that hairy men lacked wit, and so were plain dealers – straightforward.' Dromio takes 'plain dealing' to refer specifically to their behaviour towards women – the more straightforward they were in their approaches, the sooner they were in trouble.

95   *he loseth it in a kind of jollity* he has the compensation of losing it in sexual pleasure (perhaps playing on *jollity* meaning 'finery', contrasting with plainness)

96   *reason.* This word is often used punningly, with a quibble on 'raisin' or (sexually) 'raising'. Neither seems quite appropriate here, yet a double-entendre is likely. It is possible that 'raisin' was slang for 'testicle', though I have found no evidence of this.

97   *two, and sound ones, too* (an allusion to the testicles, *sound* meaning 'valid' and 'healthy')

98   *not sound* (perhaps a further pun, meaning that morally, at least, the reasons are not sound)

101   *thing* (perhaps with a quibble on *thing* meaning 'sexual organ')

102   *falsing* deceptive (including the sense 'sexually deceptive')

106   *tiring* hair-dressing
      they (his hair)

107   *porridge* soup (the original meaning)

110–11 *e'en no time* (an emendation of F's 'in no time') no time at all

114   *mend* improve

115   *bald* (punning on the meaning 'trivial', 'foolish')

118   *wafts* beckons

119   *strange* distant

120   *aspects* (accented on the second syllable) looks, expressions

127   *spake ... looked ... touched ... carved.* Each verb refers to one of the four previous lines, consecutively.

132   *better part* ('soul' or 'best qualities')

134   *fall* let fall, drop

134–8 The image recalls that used by Antipholus of Syracuse at I.2.35 (see Introduction, pages 29–30).

135   *breaking gulf* (of the waves. 'Gulf' could mean specifically a whirlpool.)

139   *dearly* grievously
      touch thee to the quick (proverbial)

141   *consecrate* (past participle)

142   *contaminate* (past participle)

145   *tear the stained skin off my harlot brow.* The idea resembles Laertes's 'brands the harlot | Even here, between the chaste unsmirchèd brow | Of my true mother' (*Hamlet*, IV.5.115–17). The brow is seen as the index to the character. There may also be an allusion to the punishment of branding.

141

148   *I know thou canst, and therefore see thou do it* (either
'I know you have the right, so do so if you hear I am
unfaithful'; or 'Because I know you could do so, I
imagine (*see*) you doing it')

149   *with* of
   blot ('stain' or 'disgrace')

153   *strumpeted by thy contagion* made a whore by contami-
nation from you

154   *Keep* if you keep

155   *unstained*. F has 'distain'd', which could make sense if
interpreted as 'dis-stained', but there is no parallel
for this elsewhere in Shakespeare, and in speaking it
would be difficult to distinguish it from 'distained'. It
is just possible that 'distained', meaning 'dishonoured',
is correct, and that Adriana is saying that by commit-
ting adultery her husband makes a whore of his wife
while keeping his own 'honour' unsullied.

156   *Plead you to me, fair dame?* 'One has never forgotten
the laughter during the Stratford-upon-Avon *Comedy
of Errors* (1962), a production, directed by Clifford
Williams, that was full of new stresses – especially
when Alec McCowen (Antipholus of Syracuse), after
listening to thirty-seven lines of fervent blank verse by
Adriana, said in bewilderment: "Plead you to *me*,
fair dame?"' (*Shakespeare's Plays Today*, Arthur
Colby Sprague and J. C. Trewin (1970), pages 71–2).

159–60   *Who ... Wants*. The syntax is difficult. *Who*, 'and I',
takes the third-person agreement in *Wants*.

161   *brother* brother-in-law

162   *wont* accustomed

166   *return* bring back, report

168   *Denied my house for his, me for his wife* denied that my
house was his, and I his wife

170   *course and drift*. The two words have the same meaning
– 'gist', 'scope'.
   compact (accented on the second syllable) agreement.
(He suspects collusion.)

176   *inspiration* (five syllables) supernatural power. Antipholus genuinely begins to suspect this.

178   *counterfeit* engage in deception
grossly obviously

179   *mood* anger

180   *Be it my wrong you are from me exempt* I must accept
the wrong you have done in cutting yourself off from
me

181   *a more contempt* even more contemptuous behaviour

182   *sleeve.* The term seems more appropriate to an
Elizabethan than to a Roman garment.

183   *Thou art an elm, my husband; I a vine.* Vines were
trained on elm trees. There are possible sources for
this image in the Bible, proverb lore, and Ovid's
Metamorphoses, which was known to Shakespeare and
where it is linked with marriage. Golding's translation
(1567) runs:

> if that the vine which runs upon the elm had not
> The tree to lean unto, it should upon the ground lie
> flat.   (XIV.665–6)

185   *with ... communicate* share

186   *possess* (more active than in modern usage) takes
possession of
from away from
it (that is, the *vine*, her *weakness*)

187   *idle* useless

188   *Who* which
with intrusion by forced entry

189   *confusion* destruction

190   *moves me for her theme* appeals to me as her subject
matter

191   *dream.* See Introduction, page 32.

193   *error* (alluding to the play's title, as also at III.2.35)

194–5   *Until ... fallacy.* Antipholus's decision derives from
Menaechmi, in which, in Warner's translation,

143

Menaechmus says: 'I'll go in with her, Messenio. I'll see further of this matter … I can lose nothing. Somewhat I shall gain, perhaps a good lodging during my abode here' (edited by Bullough, page 21).

194   *know this sure uncertainty* unravel what is certainly a mystery

195   *I'll entertain the offered fallacy* I will accept as if it were true this delusion with which I have been confronted

196   *spread* set the table

197   *beads* (prayer beads)

199   *We … sprites.* This line is metrically short. Various suggestions have been made to fill it out (see Collations, page 188), but the short line may be deliberately expressive of Dromio's consternation.

     owls (usually, perhaps rightly, emended to 'elves', on the grounds that Dromio alludes to beings that can be spoken with. But a dictionary of 1580 describes a screech-owl as a bird 'which sucked out the blood of infants lying in their cradles; a witch, that changeth the favour of children; an hag or fairy'.)

     sprites spirits

201   *pinch us black and blue.* Pinching was traditionally associated with fairies (as notably in *The Merry Wives of Windsor*, where Falstaff's punishment is to be pinched by children dressed as fairies), and Shakespeare himself frequently mentions 'fairies' and 'pinching' in the same context. E. A. Armstrong suggests that there was a subconscious associative link in his mind between the two words (*Shakespeare's Imagination* (1946), page 48). To 'pinch black and blue' was already proverbial.

203   *thou Dromio* (often emended to 'thou drone', but Luciana may be using the name as a term of contempt, perhaps with an ironical glance at its literal meaning of 'runner')

     sot blockhead

204   *transformèd*. Antipholus's fears of I.2.100 appear to be being realized. See Introduction, page 32.

208   *ape* (probably the primary meaning is figurative – 'counterfeit' – rather than literal)

210   *rides* controls, tyrannizes over
         for grass for freedom (as a horse is 'put to grass')

214   *put the finger in the eye and weep* (weep sulkily, like a child; a common expression)

215   *laughs* (the singular form of the verb with a plural subject, as commonly)

216–28 The insistent instructions to Dromio to guard the gate prepare the audience for the situation in the following scene, which otherwise might be difficult to understand.

217   *above*. See III.1, Commentary, 'Staging'.

218   *shrive you of* forgive you for, after hearing your confession
         idle frivolous

220   *forth* away from home

223   *well advised* in my right mind

225   *persever* (accented on the second syllable)

226   *mist* state of confusion
         at all adventures go take my chance, whatever the risk

1   *Staging*
     The staging of this scene presents problems. The location is before Antipholus of Ephesus's house, in which his twin is dining with Adriana and Luciana. Dromio of Syracuse is guarding the gate, with instructions to let no one enter (II.2.216 etc.). The elaborate courtesy of Antipholus's invitations to Balthasar in the first part of the scene is ironic in view of this. At line 30, Antipholus tries the door and finds it locked. Dromio of Syracuse speaks from behind the door, and so is out of sight. (However, in Clifford Williams's Stratford-upon-Avon production of 1962,

revived in 1972, both sets of actors were visible. At
the end of the previous scene Dromio of Syracuse had
mimed the outline of a door, and his own action in
locking it and pocketing the key. Thus a setting was
economically established in the minds of the audience.)
It may be that Dromio of Syracuse, Luce, and Adriana
should be out of sight of the audience throughout the
scene. But they have so much to say that this seems
clumsy. Another possibility is that some convention
should be employed whereby the audience can see
both sets of actors, but they are understood not to see
one another. There is no reason why Luce should not
come into the presence of the on-stage party, but it is
necessary that the Dromios should be kept apart, and
that Adriana should not confront her real husband at
this stage of the play. It may well be that the main
point of bringing Luce on here is to have some servant
other than Dromio to sustain the altercation. To have
Luce throw the words *What a coil is there, Dromio!
Who are those at the gate?* (line 48) behind her to an
invisible Dromio seems clumsy, and there is something to be said in favour of the suggestion that Luce
and perhaps Adriana should enter on an upper level –
the upper stage of the Elizabethan theatre. This may
be suggested by Adriana's statement that she and her
supposed husband would dine *above* (II.2.217). However, it sounds from line 57 as if Luce were expected
to be able to open the door herself, rather than simply
instruct Dromio to do so. In this edition, Dromio's
speeches are marked 'within', but not those of the
women characters. The producer is free to engineer
the scene in his own way.

2   *keep not hours* am unpunctual
4   *carcanet* jewelled necklace (the *chain* of II.1.106 and
     line 115 of this scene)
6   *face me down* maintain to my face, in spite of my denial
8   *charged* entrusted

9   *deny* disown

11–83   The verse goes into irregular trimeter couplets, used also in *Love's Labour's Lost* (for example, IV.1). Some lines have four stresses, some five, and some six.

12   *your hand* (punningly: 'your note of hand' and 'the blows dealt by your hand')

15   *I think thou art an ass.* The other Antipholus has already suspected a similar transformation in his Dromio – II.2.209.

17   *at that pass* in that predicament

19   *cheer* fare, entertainment

20   *answer* correspond to

22–3   *either at flesh or fish | A table full of welcome makes scarce one dainty dish* the warmest welcome is no substitute for even one good dish

28   *cates* provisions. It is ironical that the food being discussed is already being eaten. If simultaneous setting were employed the irony would be visually pointed.

31   *Maud, Bridget, Marian, Cicely, Gillian, Ginn.* The number of maids suggests a wealthy household; no doubt it was dictated partly by metrical requirements. *Ginn* (probably a form of 'Jenny')

32   *Mome, malthorse, capon, coxcomb, idiot, patch* (a string of insults: *mome*, blockhead, fool; *malthorse*, a heavy, brewer's horse, hence a stupid person; *capon*, eunuch; *patch*, fool)

33   *hatch* wicket, half-door (possibly with some reference to the stage furniture)

34   *conjure for* try to raise by magic
      such store such a lot, so many

35   *one is one too many* (presumably a semi-proverbial misogynist expression)

36   *stays* waits

37   *catch cold on's feet.* There was an Italian proverb 'to have a cold at the feet', meaning 'to be forced to sell cheap'. It is used by Jonson in *Volpone*, II.2.40: 'I am not, as your Lombard proverb saith, cold on my feet,

147

or content to part with my commodities at a cheaper rate than I accustomed.' Here it seems to be used in a generally abusive sense.

39   *I'll tell you when an you'll tell me wherefore.* The proverb 'There is never a why but there is a wherefore' has already been used at II.2.43–5.
      an if

42   *owe* own

43   *for this time* for the time being

45   *credit . . . blame.* It is his *name* that might have got him *credit*, his *office* (or duties) that has got him *blame*.
      mickle great

47   *Thou wouldst have changed thy face for a name, or thy name for an ass.* This is a difficult line, which has often been emended (see Collations, page 188). As it stands it might mean 'You would have been willing to exchange your *face* ('identity') for someone else's *name* (so as to evade blame), or your *name* for that of an *ass* (as an acknowledgement of the reality of the situation).' It has been suspected that *face* is a mistake for 'office', to balance with line 44, and that *a name* should read 'an aim' (an object of attack). Certainly puns are to be suspected in a passage like this; *ass* rhyming with *place* suggests one on *an ass* and 'an ace', though the joke would seem neither clear nor very uproarious.

      (stage direction) *Enter Luce.* See the note on the staging at the beginning of the scene. Luce is based on two characters in *Menaechmi*, the courtesan's maid and her cook. In Shakespeare her name changes to Nell when she is mentioned at III.2.114, partly for the sake of a pun, partly perhaps to avoid confusion with Luciana. In production it might be advisable to call her 'Nell' in lines 49 and 53.

      An alternative explanation of the double name is offered by Desmond Bland in his edition of *Gesta Grayorum.* He suggests that she was originally called

Nell throughout; but that when the play was given at
Gray's Inn her name was altered here to Luce in
allusion to a London brothel-keeper, Lucy 'Negro'
Morgan, who is mentioned in *Gesta Grayorum*.

48   *coil* row, commotion

51   *Have at you* (an expression of hostile intent)
       set in my staff (proverbial; perhaps with a bawdy
       quibble) make myself at home

52   *'When? Can you tell?'* (a defiant expression)

54, 59 *minion* hussy (used in its sense of 'darling' at II.1.87)

54   *trow* trust, suppose. This is emended for the sake of
       the rhyme from F's 'hope'. This makes a triple
       rhyme. There are others in the play (for example,
       lines 63–5 and 75–7 of this scene), but it is possible
       that F is correct and a line ending in a word rhyming
       with *hope* has dropped out. The action implied by the
       passage is not entirely clear.

55   *I thought to have asked you* (described by M. P. Tilley
       in his *Dictionary of Proverbs* as 'a mocking retort'. He
       offers one other example, from Lyly's play *Mother
       Bombie*, IV.2.36)
       And you said no (at line 49)

56   *So come – help. Well struck! There was blow for blow.*
       The action is uncertain. Perhaps Dromio of Ephesus
       gets his master to help him in beating alternately (*blow
       for blow*) at the door. Or perhaps they both beat on the
       door together, and *There was blow for blow* means 'we
       have answered their (non-physical) blows with ones of
       our own.'

58   *Let him knock till it ache* (with a bawdy quibble)

60   *and* since there is

61   *keeps* continues to make

62   *boys* (a contemptuous use) fellows

65   *If you went in pain, master, this knave would go sore*
       (may be just a roundabout way of saying 'You are the
       knave she means'; or perhaps 'If you are to be beaten,
       I, who am really a knave, shall suffer still more')

66 *cheer* food

cheer . . . nor welcome (ruefully referring back to their conversation at lines 19–29)

fain gladly

67 *In debating* having debated

part depart

68 *They* (Balthasar and Angelo. Dromio is being ironical at his master's expense, since none of them can get in.)

69 *in the wind* strange going on. (Dromio takes the phrase literally.)

71 *Your cake here is warm within* (probably an allusion to Adriana, who is *warm* because she is safely in the house, because she is eating, and because she has a lover)

72 *mad as a buck* (a proverbial description of anger)

bought and sold tricked and betrayed; 'sold'

74 *Break any breaking* (a threatening way of saying 'if you break anything'; compare *Romeo and Juliet*, III.5.152: 'Thank me no thankings, nor proud me no prouds')

75 *break a word* speak, exchange words

words are but wind (coarsely quibbled on in the next line)

77 *thou wantest breaking* you need to be beaten (or 'broken in')

hind boorish servant

79 *when fowls have no feathers, and fish have no fin* (possibly proverbial. In Warner's *Menaechmi*, Menaechmus, asked by the doctor what he drinks, replies irritably 'Why dost not as well ask me whether I eat bread, or cheese, or beef, or porridge, or birds that bear feathers, or fishes that have fins?' (edited by Bullough, page 33).)

80 *crow* crowbar

83 *sirrah* (the other Dromio)

pluck a crow (proverbial) fight it out, settle our account

87 *suspect* (accented on the second syllable) suspicion

89 *Once this* in short; to sum up

92 *excuse* explain

93	*made* shut
95	*the Tiger* (presumably an inn)
97	*restraint* keeping out
98	*offer* try
99	*stirring passage* busy traffic
100	*vulgar* public
	of on
101	*supposèd* presumed true
102	*ungallèd* uninjured, unsullied
	estimation reputation
103	*intrusion* forced entry
105	*lives upon succession* ('passes from one generation to the next' or 'keeps alive by creating new slanders to succeed itself')
106	*For ever housed where it gets possession.* The scansion is in doubt. Probably *possession* (and *succession* in the previous line) should have four syllables. Editors sometimes emend *ever* to 'e'er', giving 'For *e'er* housed *where* it *gets* possession'; other possibilities are 'For *ever* housèd *where* it *gets* possession' and 'For *ever* hous'd *where* it *gets* possession'.
108	*in despite of mirth* (perhaps 'in spite of the mockery' or 'in order to spite merriment')
109–10	*of excellent discourse,* | *Pretty and witty; wild, and yet, too, gentle.* The Courtesan's attributes are of the kind that Adriana feared that she herself lacked (II.1.89–91).
110	*wild.* The word had a wide range of possible meanings, from 'shy' to 'licentious'. Perhaps 'lively' would convey the idiomatic sense.
112	*but, I protest, without desert.* This reflects Shakespeare's problem in presenting a story based on Roman morality in a manner that would conform to the moral conventions of the literature and drama of his time. In *Menaechmi* the liaison between Menaechmus and the courtesan is certainly sexual. Shakespeare makes Antipholus refute such a suggestion; and no doubt we

are intended to believe him. See Introduction, page 19.

113   *withal* with

115   *chain* (the *carcanet* of line 4; compare II.1.106)
       this this time

116   *Porpentine.* This is the Shakespearian form of 'porcu-
pine'. Here, it is the name of the Courtesan's house.
There seem to have been both an inn and a brothel of
this name in Shakespeare's London.

117   *there's the house* that's where she lives, that's the name
of her house

117–19   *That chain will I bestow . . . Upon mine hostess there.* At
III.2.181 Angelo tells Antipholus to take the chain to
his wife. The inconsistency can be evaded by speaking
these lines aside.

120–21   *Since mine own doors refuse to entertain me,* | *I'll knock
elsewhere to see if they'll disdain me.* In ascribing
Antipholus's visit to the Courtesan to his wife's
harshness, Shakespeare mitigates his offence in a way
that is not thought necessary in *Menaechmi.* See
Introduction, page 19.

III.2   There is no time-break between the scenes. Luciana
and Antipholus of Syracuse enter from within the
house. They speak in quatrains (to line 52), which
mark the formal nature of Luciana's opening address
and are also suited to the fervour of Antipholus's
wooing of her.

      (*stage direction*) *Luciana.* F reads '*Iuliana*', with '*Iulia*'
in the speech prefix. This is perhaps a mistake in
Shakespeare's manuscript. 'Julia' is a character in *The
Two Gentlemen of Verona.*

2–4   *Shall . . . ruinous.* F reads:

                   shall *Antipholus*
    Euen in the spring of Loue, thy Loue-springs rot?
    Shall loue in buildings grow so ruinate?

'Buildings' is always emended to 'building'. Lines 2
and 4 need to rhyme. The alternative to the solution
adopted here is to add 'hate' at the end of line 2,
reading 'Shall, Antipholus, hate . . .'; but 'ruinate'
occurs elsewhere in Shakespeare only as a verb.

3   *love-springs* young 'shoots' of love

4   *love in building grow so ruinous* the buildings of love
become so ruinous. In *The Two Gentlemen of Verona*
Valentine wishes that Silvia would come to the
'mansion' of his breast 'Lest, growing ruinous, the
building fall' (V.4.7–10).

7–28   These sophistical arguments sound oddly on Luciana's
lips. They closely resemble those in a poem from
Ovid's *Amores* (III.xiv; III.xiii in Marlowe's translation), with which Shakespeare appears to have been
eking out his invention. Compare, for instance, lines
15–16:

> Be secret-false – what need she be acquainted?
>   What simple thief brags of his own attaint?

with Ovid (Marlowe's translation, lines 7–8):

> What madness is't to tell night's pranks by day,
>   And hidden secrets openly to bewray?

8   *Muffle* hide. (The next line picks up the sense of
'blindfold'.)
    blindness concealment

10   *orator* spokesman

11   *become disloyalty* put a good front on your infidelity

12   *harbinger* herald

14   *carriage* bearing

16   *What simple thief brags* what thief is so foolish as to
brag
    attaint disgrace

17   *truant with your bed* be unfaithful. Luciana assumes
that Antipholus of Syracuse has committed the crime

of which Antipholus of Ephesus has just declared himself innocent (III.1.112).

18   *at board* at the table

19   *bastard fame* illegitimate honour

20   *is* (the singular form of the verb with a plural subject, as commonly)

22   *compact of credit* made up entirely of trust

23   *Though others have the arm, show us the sleeve.* At II.2.182 Adriana has said that she will *fasten on* her husband's sleeve, seeking strength from him. Luciana, who was present on that occasion, now picks up the same image.

24   *motion* (a technical term for the movements of heavenly bodies) orbit

27   *vain* false

29   *your name is else* other name you have

30   *of* on

32   *our earth's wonder.* This has been supposed to refer to Queen Elizabeth.

34   *conceit* apprehension

35   *errors.* This picks up the play's title again, as at II.2.193.

36   *folded* hidden

37   *Against my soul's pure truth why labour you* why are you labouring against my soul's knowledge of the simple truth

40   *Transform.* The imagery of metamorphosis, begun with references to the Dromios' transformation into asses (II.2.209 and III.1.18; see also line 77 of this scene), is now transferred to a higher plane with the idea of Antipholus's being willing to transform himself for Luciana's sake. See Introduction, page 32.

43   *Nor . . . no* (a double negative; *no* reinforces *Nor*)

44   *decline* incline

45   *train* entice, lure

45–52   *mermaid . . . drown . . . flood . . . siren . . . waves . . . drownèd . . . sink.* The idea of loss of identity through drowning (here presented as a desirable fate when undergone for the sake of love) refers back to the sea imagery in which this same Antipholus had figured his search for his mother and brother (I.2.35–40) and in which Adriana, addressing him, had imaged her identity with him (II.2.134–8). See Introduction, pages 29–30.

45 *note* song (alluding to the legend of mermaids luring sailors to destruction by their song)

49 *as . . . take* take for, take as if you were

bed. The image seems a little far-fetched, and, as *bed* is an emendation for F's 'bud', must be somewhat suspect. But it gains support from *lie*, and the generally erotic connotations of *bed*, *lie*, and (in this passage) *die*.

thee (often emended to 'them', that is, her hairs)

51 *death . . . die* (the common image of the consummation of love as a dying)

52 *Let love, being light, be drownèd if she sink.* Love is *light*, so, if she sinks in these circumstances, will be proved not truly to be love. A similar idea is expressed in Shakespeare's *Venus and Adonis* (lines 149–50):

> Love is a spirit all compact of fire,
> Not gross to sink, but light, and will aspire.

light (playing on the senses of 'wanton' and 'buoyant')

54 *mated* (both 'astounded' and 'partnered')

55 *a fault that springeth from your eye* (perhaps with the suggestion that Antipholus's emotions, springing only from the sight, are shallow)

58 *wink* close one's eyes

61 *thyself, mine own self's better part.* Adriana had used the same words to this Antipholus at II.2.132.

64 *My sole earth's heaven, and my heaven's claim* my only heaven on earth, and the only claim on heaven I shall ever have

66 *Call thyself sister, sweet, for I am thee* call yourself your

own sister, because I am identified with you as you think I should be with her

70   *good will* approval. It is uncertain whether the actress should play this as indicating sudden acceptance, or as a stratagem to escape from an embarrassing situation. When Luciana reports to her sister, it is clear that she had been attracted by Antipholus (see IV.2.14–16).

78   *besides* (punningly)

82   *One that claims me.* Dromio's experiences with the kitchen wench parallel his master's with Adriana (II.2).

83   *have* (with a sexual sense)

87–8   *a beast.* Elizabethan pronunciation suggests a pun on 'abased'.

93–4   *sir-reverence* (a corruption of 'save-your-reverence', a phrase of apology for saying something that might cause offence. It was also a euphemism for 'dung'.)

99   *grease* (punning on 'grace')

102   *a Poland winter* for as long as winter lasts in Poland

103   *week* (possibly with a pun on 'wick')

106   *Swart* swarthy, dark

107   *sweats a man* (an elliptical way of saying 'sweats so much that a man')

111   *in grain* inherent

115   *ell* (a measure of one-and-a-quarter yards)

120–21   *I could find out countries in her.* Harry Levin comments: 'it is by no means a far-fetched gag, since it embodies – on a more than miniature scale – the principal contrast of the play: on the one hand, extensive voyaging; on the other, intensive domesticity' (Signet edition, Introduction, page xxxii).

125   *bogs* (bawdy; it is not certain whether *bog* meant 'privy' in Shakespeare's time)

130–31   *armed and reverted, making war against her heir.* This is one of the most discussed passages of the play, being based on an uncertain topical allusion. *Heir* obviously puns on 'hair'. Henry III of France died in 1589; the *heir* who had to fight for his right against the Catholic

League was Henry of Navarre, crowned Henry IV in February 1594. However, France was in a state of civil war for some years before 1589 and after 1594, so the passage is not much help in dating the play. Dr Johnson pointed also to a bawdy allusion here, inferring that Nell bore the marks of venereal disease: 'By a forehead "armed", he means covered with incrusted eruptions; by "reverted", he means having the hair turning backward.'

131   *reverted* revolted, in rebellion

133   *chalky cliffs* (the cliffs of Dover; teeth)

135   *salt rheum* (watery discharge from the eyes or nose; the English Channel; possibly punning also on the 'rhumb' lines on a map)

139   *hot* (referring to Spanish spices)

140   *the Indies* (the West Indies, a source of wealth especially to Spain (line 143))

141–2   *all o'er embellished* embellished all over

142   *carbuncles* (in Shakespeare's day, as now, inflammations of the skin as well as jewels)

142–3   *declining their rich aspect to* looking down on (perhaps implying a hooked nose)

144   *armadoes* (the usual early form) armadas, fleets (usually of warships)
         carracks galleons, large merchant ships
         ballast (past participle of the verb) loaded

145   *Belgia* (used loosely for the area including Holland and the present Belgium)

147   *so low.* (The Netherlands were the Low Countries.)

148   *diviner* witch

149   *assured* betrothed

150   *privy* secret
         of on

154   *a curtal dog* (a dog with a docked tail; a household dog)
         turn i' the wheel (tread, as dogs did, a wheel operating a spit)

155   *hie thee* hasten

155   *presently* immediately
        Post hasten
        road harbour
156   *An if* if
164   *witches*. (The word was used of both sexes.) See Intro-
        duction, page 33.
168   *with* of
        sovereign excellent
171   *to* of
172   *I'll stop mine ears against the mermaid's song* (as
        Ulysses, in the *Odyssey*, stopped his men's ears with
        wax so that they might not be beguiled by the sirens.
        Antipholus had called Luciana a mermaid at line 45.)
175   *ta'en you* overtaken you, encountered you
176   *stay* delay
178   *What please* what it may please
181   *please your wife withal*. See Commentary to III.1.117–
        19.
182   *soon at*. See Commentary to I.2.26.
188   *vain* foolish
190   *shifts* tricks
193   *straight* immediately

IV.1   (stage direction) *Second Merchant*. In F he is not
        distinguished from the Merchant of I.2. But they
        appear to be different, as the one in I.2 knows the ways
        of the city and its inhabitants, whereas this one has to
        ask about Antipholus *How is the man esteemed here in
        the city?* (V.1.4).
1   *Pentecost* (Whitsuntide)
2   *since* since then
3   *Nor ... I had not* (a double negative, *not* reinforcing
        Nor) and I should not have
4   *Persia* (with which there was much trade in Shake-
        speare's time)
        guilders. See Commentary to I.1.8.

5	*present satisfaction* immediate payment

5   *present satisfaction* immediate payment

6   *attach* arrest

7   *Even just* precisely

8   *growing* growing due

10 *five o'clock.* See Commentary to I.2.26.

12 *Pleaseth you* if you please to

13 (stage direction) *from the Courtesan's.* This is Shake-speare's direction, and probably indicates that he thought of the play's staging as suggested in the Introduction, page 25.

16 *rope's end* (used for flogging)

21 *I buy a thousand pound a year, I buy a rope.* The joke has not been explained, which is particularly tiresome as the actor needs to make something of his exit-line. But if spoken with conviction the line can raise an uncomprehending laugh. Dromio may be saying that he is as willing to obey his master's command (to buy a rope) as he would be to receive a thousand pounds a year.

22 *holp up* helped

25 *Belike* perhaps

27 *Saving* with respect for

28 *utmost* last

29 *chargeful* costly
      fashion workmanship

30 *ducats* (gold coins)

32 *presently* immediately

34 *present* ready, available

41 *time enough* soon enough, in time

43 *An if* if

46 *Both wind and tide stays for this gentleman* (a variation of the proverb 'Time and tide stay for no man')
      stays (the singular form of the verb with a plural subject, as commonly)

47 *too blame* (a common sixteenth- and seventeenth-century usage) too blameworthy

48 *dalliance* idle talk, fooling

51   *shrew*. The word could be used of a person of either
        sex.

56   *me by some token* me with some evidence (by which I
        can collect the money)

57   *run this humour out of breath* take the joke too far

60   *answer* pay

68   *stands upon* concerns

69   *at my suit* on my petition

72   *touches* injures

74   *attach* arrest

75   *that* that which

77   *fee*. Public officers were entitled to a fee for the
        exercise of their functions.

79   *apparently* blatantly

80   *I do arrest you, sir*. The Officer is now in the odd
        situation of having two men under arrest, one at the
        suit of the other.

85   (stage direction) *from the bay*. The direction (unlike
        the one at line 13) seems to be literary rather than
        theatrical, since the 'bay' would not be represented.
        It derives from the Plautine convention that one side
        of the stage leads to the bay or harbour, the other to
        the city.

86   *of Epidamnum*. At I.2.1 Antipholus had been advised
        to pretend that he came from Epidamnum, not
        Syracuse.

88   *then she*. F reads 'then sir she'. Perhaps 'sir' crept in
        accidentally, but it is also possible that Shakespeare
        wrote the irregular line, which would not sound odd
        in the mouth of the breathless Dromio.
        bears away leaves
        fraughtage freight, luggage

90   *balsamum* balm
        aqua-vitae spirits. These details are oddly circum-
        stantial. Perhaps the aqua-vitae is intended as a
        consolation in case of sea-sickness.

91   *in her trim* ready to sail

93   *master*. This may be Dromio's form of address to Antipholus, or he may mean that the ship is waiting for its *master*, or captain.

94-5   *sheep . . . ship* (a common pun; the words were closer in pronunciation than now)

96   *hire* (two syllables)
        waftage passage

99   *You sent me for a rope's end as soon.* This short line is usually, perhaps correctly, filled out to read 'end, sir, as . . .'. But if it is taken as a muttered protest some irregularity is effective.
        a rope's end (a beating, or perhaps a halter. Dromio of Ephesus, of course, really had been sent to buy a rope's end.)

102   *list* listen to

105   *Turkish tapestry.* In Elizabethan England, needlework imitations of Eastern carpets were used for window-seats, cushions, and so on. This seems to be the kind of thing that Shakespeare has in mind here.

111   *Dowsabel* (a general term for a sweetheart, from the Italian *Dulcibella* or French *Douce et belle*; here used ironically for Nell)

112   *compass* ('embrace', and 'win')

2.1-4   The scene begins with a quatrain, the verse form employed in the interview that Luciana is here reporting (III.2.1-52); though this episode then continues in couplets, it is rounded off with another quatrain (lines 25-8), as is the scene (lines 62-5).

2   *austerely* objectively, without being affected by what he said. An alternative interpretation is 'by the austerity'. The word has been amended to 'a surety'. In the light of *earnest* in the next line this is plausible, but unnecessary.

4   *or . . . or* (a common use, intensifying the antithesis)

161

5   *observation*. The following image shows that this carries the technical sense of 'observing the heavens'.

6   *heart's meteors tilting* conflicting emotions. 'Meteors' are any kind of luminous appearance in the sky; *tilting* images them fighting against one another as at a formal combat.

7   *no* (emphatic) any

8   *spite* annoyance

9   *stranger* foreigner

10   *And true he swore, though yet forsworn he were.* Presumably Adriana means that although this has not been true so far, it certainly will be in the future; or perhaps rather that he is certainly behaving like a stranger, though he is a liar to claim that he is one.

16   *speak him fair* speak kindly to him, encourage him

18   *his* its

19   *sere* withered, dried up

20   *shapeless* unshapely, ugly

21   *ungentle* ungentlemanly, unchivalrous

22   *Stigmatical* of deformed appearance
        making the way he is made physically

26   *yet* still (not 'nevertheless')
        would herein others' eyes were worse (so that they would not see his faults: an admission that she still loves him)

27   *Far from her nest the lapwing cries away* (an allusion to the lapwing's (or peewit's) proverbial – and actual – method of diverting intruders away from its nest. Adriana refers to the division between what she says and what she feels.)

29   *Here, go – the desk, the purse, sweet, now, make haste.* Dromio in his haste speaks incoherently, either to himself, remembering his instructions, or to Adriana, trying to convey the gist of his message. Editors have often emended *sweet*. J. Dover Wilson, in his New Cambridge edition (1922), read 'sweat', and was followed by R. A. Foakes in the new Arden edition

(1962); but Wilson reverted to 'sweet' when his edition was reprinted, in 1962. Justifying the emendation, he wrote: 'The rude clown can hardly address the ladies as "sweet" . . .'. It seems no less indecorous for him to tell them to sweat. If addressed to Adriana, *sweet* need mean no more than the terms of endearment often addressed to their clients by bus conductors and shop assistants.

32   *Tartar limbo*. 'Limbo' was often used for 'prison', and also for 'hell', though more properly it is an adjacent area. *Tartar* is an abbreviation of 'Tartarus', the infernal prison of classical mythology, but must also have suggested 'Tartars', regarded as savage.

33   *everlasting* (the name of a material used for the uniform of prison officers)

34   *hard heart is buttoned up with steel* (presumably alluding to some feature of the prison officer's dress)

35   *fairy*. Many editors adopt the emendation of the eighteenth-century editor Lewis Theobald, 'fury', on which Dr Johnson's comment seems still appropriate: 'Mr Theobald seems to have forgotten that there were fairies like "hobgoblins", pitiless and rough, and described as malevolent and mischievous. His emendation is, however, plausible.'

36   *buff* (buff-leather, used for the uniform of sergeants and other officials)

37   *backfriend* false friend (with a reference to the sergeant's clapping people on the back as he arrests them)
        shoulder-clapper (an arresting officer)
        countermands prohibits (probably with a pun on the 'Counter', a name given to various debtors' prisons)

38   *passages of* movement of people in
        creeks winding lanes
        lands. The word is difficult to explain, but may be a form of 'launds', meaning 'glades' or, more generally, 'strips of land'. In *3 Henry VI*, III.1.2, a Keeper says 'through this laund anon the deer will come'. If the

word had hunting associations for Shakespeare, this might have suggested the image in line 39. Emendation to 'lanes' would be tempting were it not for the rhyme.

39   *runs counter* (a hunting term, meaning 'runs in the direction opposite to that of the prey', with an allusion to the name of the debtors' prisons)
       draws dryfoot (a hunting term, meaning 'follows the prey simply by the scent of its foot')

40   *Judgement* (1) in a court of law; (2) the Day of Judgement
       hell (1) prison (the name of a particular debtors' prison under Westminster Hall); (2) (in its literal sense)

41–2   *matter ... matter.* An obscure, possibly strained, legal pun seems likely; perhaps the second *matter* plays on the word as a subject of dispute formulated in a *case*.

42   *on the case* (punningly of (1) a law term, now obsolete, used of particular cases, and (2) *case* meaning 'clothes': the sergeant's hand descending on his victim's shoulder)

45   *is* (a common ellipsis) he is

46   *redemption* ransom, the means to redeem himself. The phrase has sometimes been printed as 'Mistress Redemption' on the assumption that Adriana is being seen as a semi-abstract character such as might have appeared in a Morality play.

49–50 *band ... band* (quibbling on 'bond' (of which *band* is another form), and *band* as 'neckband' or 'ruff')

51   *chain.* Antipholus was arrested for money owing on a chain, such as would have been worn round the neck (see V.1.258–9); and also a chain was used to arrest him.

53   *It was two ere I left him, and now the clock strikes one.* The point of this line depends on a pun obscured by the passage of time. 'On' and 'one' were pronounced identically. Dromio says that the clock strikes on, but Adriana understands him to mean 'one'. The line

epitomizes the confusion of time so common in the play. See Introduction, page 35.

55, 61   *hour.* A pun on 'whore' has been suggested, but one on 'ower' would make better sense.

55   *sergeant* (the proper title of the officer responsible for making arrests and delivering summonses)
  'a he

56   *fondly* foolishly

57   *Time . . . owes more than he's worth to season.* A pun on *season* has been suspected, perhaps as 'seisin', a legal term meaning 'possession as of freehold', perhaps as 'seizing', though neither seems to make a successful joke. Perhaps there is a double pun on *Time*/'thyme' and *season* as 'season (of the year)' and 'seasoning': 'Time . . . owes more than his value as seasoning'. Gāmini Salgādo writes: 'S. Dromio's cryptic line . . . has often been taken to mean "There is never enough time to do all that occasion offers" but it could equally easily, and with perhaps greater relevance, be understood as saying that time has so exhausted itself that it's more trouble than it's worth to set it straight ("season" neatly combining the two usual senses of "bring to maturity" and "make palatable or agreeable"). Alternatively . . . S. Dromio may be saying that time in itself is empty and owes all his powers and more to "season" the harmonious cyclical regularity of the natural world.'

59   *time comes stealing on by night and day* (proverbial)

60–61   *If 'a be in debt and theft, and a sergeant in the way, | Hath he not reason to turn back an hour in a day?* The game of wit returns to its starting point, the notion that the hours are turning back (lines 54–5). 'If time is in debt, and also a thief, and meets a sergeant, hasn't he good reason to retreat to the extent of an hour in a day?'

60   *and theft* (and a thief – line 58)

62   *straight* immediately

64   *pressed down with* overburdened with, depressed by
64, 65 *conceit* imagination (a *comfort* because of what is to
        come, an *injury* because imagination has caused her
        unhappiness)

IV.3.1 *salute* greet
4   *tender* offer
5   *other* (a normal plural) others
9   *therewithal* thereupon, forthwith
10   *imaginary wiles* tricks existing only in the imagination
11   *Lapland sorcerers.* Lapland was notorious for sorcery.
13–14   *What, have you got the picture of old Adam new-
        apparelled?* The meaning of this is uncertain, and it
        has been variously, though unconvincingly, emended
        (see Collations, page 188). Dromio may be saying 'Is
        the sergeant still with you?' or 'Have you got rid of
        the sergeant?' *The picture of* seems to mean, as we
        might say, 'that "image" of', 'that man who really
        seems to be (old Adam)'. *Old Adam* is 'offending'
        Adam, who was not *apparelled* till he had sinned. So
        the question might be paraphrased 'Have you still got
        that image of sinful man in your company?' If this
        seems excessively circuitous, it may be so simply in
        order to release a series of puns. But it is possible that
        word-play lies behind the question itself. If the mean-
        ing is 'Have you got rid of the sergeant?' it would
        depend on submerged puns. Adam, before the Fall,
        was dressed in 'buff' – naked – and officers of the law
        wear buff – leather clothing. If the sergeant put on
        different clothing he would take on a new 'suit' – or
        'case' – and so leave Antipholus. The full complexity
        of this is scarcely susceptible to paraphrase, but the
        general sense would be 'Have you managed to get the
        sergeant, who resembled old Adam in wearing buff,
        into another "suit"?'
16–17   *the paradise.* The definite article suggests a topical

allusion to an inn or something of the kind kept by a man called Adam; but this is unverifiable.

18   *the calf's skin that was killed for the prodigal* (that is, the skin of the calf that was killed for the prodigal son, Luke 15.11–32; alluding to the sergeant's leather clothes, and with an ironical glance at his function of arresting debtors, who have been 'prodigal')

19   *like an evil angel.* Behind this phrase may lie a memory of Acts 12.8–12, in which a good angel appears to Peter in prison, smites him on the side, and releases him.

20   *forsake your liberty.* Various levels of punning are possible: 'give up your freedom'; 'leave your domain'; 'cease your wrong behaviour'; even 'sell your soul'.

23   *case of leather* (the leather case of a bass viol, and the suit (*case*) of leather worn by the sergeant)

24   *sob* respite (technically used of horses: a rest given to enable them to recover their wind)

25   *rests* (punning on 'arrests')

     decayed ruined (financially, and in opposition to *durance*)

26   *suits of durance* clothes that will last, suitable for a long term of imprisonment

     durance (both 'a hard-wearing cloth', which Shakespeare seems to have confused with 'buff', and 'imprisonment')

     sets up his rest is determined (an expression from gambling, meaning 'stakes his all'; here sustaining the pun on *rest* and 'arrest')

27   *mace* (the sergeant's staff of office)

     morris-pike (a kind of pike supposed to be of Moorish origin)

30   *band* (of officers; and punning on 'bond')

33   *rest* (punningly again)

35   *ships puts.* The second Folio (1632) reads 'ship', which may be correct; but this is a possible piece of Elizabethan syntax.

40   *hoy* (a small coasting-vessel, jokingly named, especially since a *hoy* was intended for fast sailing)

angels (gold coins worth up to ten shillings and bearing a figure of St Michael overcoming the dragon. There may be a reference to Acts 12.11: 'that the Lord hath sent his angel, and hath delivered me' (that is, Peter, from prison).)

42   *distract* distracted, mad

44   (stage direction) *Courtesan.* Her identity is not established for the audience in the dialogue. She may have entered by a door marked 'The Porpentine', or with its sign – see III.1.116, and Introduction, page 25. She should not, as in some modern productions, be portrayed as a blatant prostitute. See Introduction, page 19.

48   *Satan, avoid!* Compare Matthew 4.10, 'Avoid Satan'; quoted in the Gospel for the first Sunday in Lent.

avoid! be off!

51–2   *Nay ... dam.* This will scan as a verse line, and the way it is set up in F may suggest that it was thought of as one.

52   *devil's dam* (literally 'devil's mother': a phrase used derogatively of a woman)

habit costume

light immoral (with perhaps a hint of the 'light' of Lucifer, certainly present in the following use of the word)

54   *as much to say* (a normal construction, often emended to 'as much as to say')

55–6   *It is written they appear to men like angels of light.* The phrase 'It is written' is common in the Gospels. 2 Corinthians 11.14 has 'for Satan himself is transformed into an angel of light', which with variations became proverbial. Thomas Nashe, in *The Terrors of the Night* (1594), wrote: 'It is not to be gainsaid but the devil can transform himself into an angel of light ...' (edited by R. B. McKerrow, I.347).

57   *burn* (that is, infect with venereal disease)
59   *mend* supplement, complete
      here (pointing, presumably, to the door of her house)
60–61 *spoon-meat* (soft food for children or invalids: used to
      introduce the following proverbial expression)
61   *bespeak* order
63–4 *he must have a long spoon that must eat with the devil*
      (proverbial; defined in 1552 as 'he which must have to
      do with crafty persons ought himself to know craft':
      M. P. Tilley, *Dictionary of Proverbs*, S.771)
65   *then* (often, quite plausibly, emended to 'thou')
      What why
66   *you . . . all* (in Ephesus)
67   *conjure* charge (the technical term for addressing
      spirits; actors sometimes accompany the phrase with
      ritualistic gestures)
68   *at dinner*. That Antipholus of Ephesus has dined with
      the Courtesan has not been previously mentioned in
      the dialogue, but the stage direction to IV.1.13 refers
      to his leaving her house. All this supports the theory
      that the house should be readily identifiable on the
      stage, perhaps by means of the sign of the Porpentine.
69   *for my diamond* in return for my diamond (ring)
71–6 These lines, printed as prose in F, hover uncertainly
      between verse and prose.
71   *ask* (that is, in return for not troubling people)
71–3 *parings . . . cherry stone*. These are objects that might
      have been used in witchcraft. Witches often gave a
      drop of blood to their familiar spirit in return for his
      services.
75   *an if* if
76   *The devil will shake her chain*. Compare Revelation
      20.1–2: 'And I saw an angel come down from heaven,
      having the key of the bottomless pit, and a great chain
      in his hand. And he took the dragon, that old serpent,
      which is the devil and Satanas, and he bound him a
      thousand years.'

169

79   *Avaunt* be off!

80   *'Fly pride', says the peacock*. The peacock was itself a traditional personification of pride, therefore ill qualified to instruct others to eschew it. Dromio is commenting obliquely on the irony in the Courtesan's asking Antipholus not to cheat her, since he believes that the devil is speaking through her, and thus she is cheating them.

82   *demean himself* behave

87   *rage* madness

91   *way* entrance

92   *My way* (the best thing for *me* to do)
       hie hasten
       home (in the sense of 'directly', as we might say 'to strike *home*')

94   *perforce* forcibly

95   *I fittest choose* I choose as the most appropriate

IV.4   (stage direction) *Officer*. F has '*Iailor*', but presumably this is the Officer of IV.1.

2-3   *so . . . as* as . . . as

3   *To warrant thee* as security

4   *wayward* perverse, awkward

5   *lightly* readily

6   *should be attached* should have been arrested

9, 10   *that* that which

10   *pay* (with a beating)

14   *serve you . . . five hundred at the rate* provide you with five hundred at that price

19   *'tis for me to be patient. I am in adversity* (alluding to Psalm 94.13: 'That thou mayst give him patience in time of adversity')

20   *Good now* (an expression of entreaty)

26   *sensible in nothing but blows* responsive to nothing but violence

28   *ears* (playing on 'years', as the next sentence shows;

'years' seems to have been a common pronunciation of 'ears'. The word-play survives in the still current expression 'for donkey's years'.)

0–32 *When I am . . . beating.* Again, verse characteristics enter Dromio's prose.

5 *wont* is accustomed to do

7 (stage direction) *Pinch.* A detailed, though subjective, description of him is given at V.1.238–42. The description of him as a *schoolmaster* in the stage direction is presumably Shakespeare's. At line 45 he is referred to as a *conjuror*, alluding to his power to use Latin, the ordinary language of teaching, in the attempt to exorcize spirits. His title of Doctor alludes to his qualification as a schoolmaster, not a physician.

9–41 *respice finem* – 'respect your end', or rather, to prophesy like the parrot, 'beware the rope's end'. Two jokes lie behind this. One is a pun, found elsewhere, on the tag *respice finem* meaning 'think of your end', and *respice funem*, 'think of a rope' – that is, of an end by hanging. The other is a trick of teaching parrots to say 'rope'. Dromio is ruefully warning Adriana of the use to which Antipholus means to put the rope.

2 *still* continually, incessantly

5 *conjuror* (one who exorcized the devils that caused madness)

7 *please* satisfy with

9 *ecstasy* fit of madness

4 *straight* immediately

8 *minion* (used contemptuously of a loose woman)

) *companion* (used contemptuously)

2 *denied* not allowed

5 *slanders* (could mean 'disgraceful actions' as well as 'disgraces')

7–75 *sooth to say . . . Perdie . . . Sans fable . . . Certes . . . In verity.* This string of mild and old-fashioned oaths seems designed to mock as well as to *humour* (line 79) Antipholus.

69 *Perdie* indeed, by God!

71 *Sans* (the French word, often used in Elizabethan English) without

73 *Certes* certainly
  vestal maid (with an allusion to 'her charge being like that of the vestal virgins, to keep the fire burning', as Dr Johnson wrote)

75 *bears* (the singular form of the verb with a plural subject, as commonly)

77 *soothe* humour
  contraries lies

78 *fellow* (Dromio)
  finds his vein understands his (master's) frame of mind. Pinch mistakenly supposes that Dromio is merely humouring his master.

83–4 *Heart and good will ... But ... not a rag of money.* This seems to have been a semi-proverbial expression. *a rag of money* was a farthing.

90 *both man and master is possessed.* Pinch no longer believes that Dromio is merely humouring his master
  is (acceptable Elizabethan grammar)

92 *They must be bound and laid in some dark room.* This seems to have been an accepted treatment for madness, as in *Twelfth Night*, III.4.134–5.

93 *forth* out

104 (stage direction) *Enter three or four and offer to bind him. He strives.* The imprecision (*three or four*) in this direction suggests that it was written by Shakespeare, not the stage manager, who would need to know exactly how many attendants should enter. In F it is printed after line 103. The necessary business seems to be that Antipholus menaces Adriana, and when she shrieks *bind him, bind him*, some men enter to restrain him; others might enter as Pinch says *More company*. The director has some freedom of invention here.

109 *make a rescue* (take someone forcibly out of legal custody)

11   *his.* F reads 'this'. The emendation was suggested by
      S. A. Tannenbaum, 'Notes on *The Comedy of Errors*',
      Shakespeare Jahrbuch 68 (1932). Though not essential,
      it is very attractive.

12   *peevish.* This word had a range of meanings including
      'silly' and 'spiteful'; it was generally expressive of
      hostility.

14   *displeasure* offence, wrong

15–16 *He is my prisoner. If I let him go | The debt he owes will*
      be required of me. In Elizabethan times the gaoler could
      be held responsible for his prisoner's debts.

17   *discharge* pay

19   *knowing how the debt grows* when I know to what the
      debt amounts (or 'how it has arisen')

23   *entered in bond* (punningly: (1) 'tied up'; (2) 'pledged')

24   *mad* exasperate

26   *Cry 'the devil!'* (1) relieve your anger by swearing by
      the devil; (2) call on the devil supposed to be within
      you

27   *God help* (an interjection, roughly equivalent to 'Good
      God!', or 'Dear me!')
      idly foolishly

35   *Whenas* when

41   *at large* in full detail

43   *come* (probably to be understood as the past participle,
      not the active verb)
      naked swords swords drawn

44   (stage direction) In F, one column of print ends:

Let's call more helpe to haue them bound againe.
                                     Runne all out.

The next column begins:

Off. Away, they'l kill vs.
              Exeunt omnes, as fast as may be, frighted.

This edition follows R. A. Foakes's suggestion that the
direction in the manuscript was '*Runne all out, as fast*

as may be, frighted', and that it followed 'kill vs.', but
that in the printing house it accidentally split, and the
words 'Exeunt omnes' were added by a compositor to
make sense of an incomplete sentence.

146   *would be your wife* claimed to be your wife

147   *stuff* belongings

149   *Faith* (an exclamation of no very precise significance)

149,   The tide begins to turn; Dromio, at least, is willing
153–4 to stay in Ephesus. See Introduction, page 23.

150   *speak us fair* speak kindly to us

V.1.1   *hindered*. This refers to the opening episode of IV.1.

2   *of* from

8   *His word might bear my wealth*. Dover Wilson, in his
New Cambridge edition, says that this is 'not satisfactorily explained'. It seems to mean 'he could
borrow all my money merely on the strength of his
credit'.

9   (stage direction) The form of the direction in F
('*Enter Antipholus and Dromio againe*') suggests that
the action between the end of IV.4 and the beginning
of V.1 was continuous.

10   *self* same

11   *forswore* denied

12   *to me* (often emended to 'with me'. But *to* is acceptable
if we assume that Angelo is asking the Merchant for his
support.)

16   *circumstance* detailed argument

18   *imprisonment*. The Second Merchant had had Angelo
arrested at IV.1.69–71. We are not offered an explanation of how Angelo came to be released, and on good
terms with the Merchant.

20   *staying on* delaying because of

29   *impeach* accuse

31   *presently* immediately, here and now
      stand submit yourself to the test

32 (stage direction) *others* (the attendants whom Adriana instructs to bind Antipholus and Dromio)

34 *within him* inside his guard

36 *take* enter for refuge

37 *spoiled* ruined, destroyed

45 *This week* (throughout this week)

sad grave, melancholy

46 *much, much*. F reads simply 'much', which may be what Shakespeare wrote. But there is a parallel to 'much, much' in *The Merchant of Venice*, III.2.61; it is easy to see how one of the repeated words could have been omitted; and there seems no dramatic point in the short line.

47 *passion* (three syllables) disorder

49 *wrack of sea* shipwreck

51 *Strayed* led astray. (This transitive usage is unique in Shakespeare.)

62 *copy* theme

conference conversation

65 *Alone* when we were by ourselves

66 *glanced at*. F reads 'glanced', which some editors retain, with a stressed '-ed'. Shakespeare uses 'glance at' in *A Midsummer Night's Dream*, II.1.75, and in *Julius Caesar*, I.2.317, in both cases with a sense of 'allude reproachfully to'. It seems likely that 'at' was accidentally omitted.

67 *Still* continually, constantly

67–8 The rhyme stresses the Abbess's volte-face. On this passage, see Introduction, page 28.

69 *venom* (commonly used as an adjective)

70 *Poisons* (the singular form of the verb with a plural subject, as commonly)

77 *sports* recreations

79 *But moody and dull melancholy*. The line is one syllable short, and editors sometimes pad it out, for example, as 'moody, heavy, and dull ...'. But *moody* and *dull* can be spoken with such weight as to create

the illusion of a full line. (E. A. Abbott, in *A Shake-spearian Grammar* (1869 etc., ¶ 484), classes *dull* among 'monosyllables containing diphthongs and vowels [that], since they naturally allow the voice to rest upon them, are often so emphasized as to dispense with an unaccented syllable.')

82 *distemperatures* ailments, disorders

84 *or ... or* either ... or

86 *Hath* (the singular form of the verb with a plural subject, as commonly)

88 *demeaned* behaved

90 *betray me to my own reproof* trick me into recognizing my own faults

94 *took* (as in line 36)

 sanctuary. In Shakespeare's time it was still possible to take refuge from the law in a church or other sacred building.

97 *assaying* attempting

99 *office* duty (by her marriage vows)

100 *attorney* substitute

103 *approvèd* tested

105 *formal* normal

106 *branch and parcel* part and parcel

117 *perforce* forcibly

118 *By this* (by this time)

 five. The time appointed for the resolution of business affairs (I.2.26 and IV.1.10) is now named as the hour also fixed for Egeon's execution. See Introduction, page 35.

119 *Anon* soon

121 *sorry* sorrowful

129 (stage direction) *barehead* (ready for execution)

 Headsman (no doubt immediately recognizable from his costume, and perhaps carrying an axe)

132 *tender* ('care about' or 'pity')

137 *Who* (for 'whom', as often in Shakespeare)

138 *important* urgent (importunate)

letters. There is a piece of submerged narrative here. The probable explanation is that Adriana is supposed to have been the Duke's ward, and that he exercised his right of choosing a husband for her.

140 *That* with the result that

desperately with reckless violence

142 *displeasure* offence, wrong

144 *rage did like* madness took a fancy to

146 *take order for* take steps to settle

148 *wot* know

strong escape (escape involving the exercise of great strength)

151 *ireful* angry, wrathful

152 *bent* (the past participle rather than the past tense) turned

156 *gates.* This suggests the use of a stage door for the entrance to the abbey. See also line 37.

160 *help* treatment

165–6 *Go . . . me.* Presumably some servants begin to execute the Duke's order, but are interrupted by the entrance of the Messenger. The Duke again gives instructions for the Abbess to be called in at line 281.

167 *determine* settle

168 *shift* escape

170 *a-row* one after the other (in a row)

171–3 *beard . . . hair.* There is some resemblance here to Marlowe's *Edward II*, in which the King is forcibly washed with puddle water and shaved (V.3). Later he complains that he has had to stand 'in mire and puddle'. Marlowe was working from historical sources, so if there is any influence, it is probably from him to Shakespeare. His play has not been precisely dated, but cannot be later than 1593.

173 *puddled* stirred up, filthy

174 *My master preaches patience to him, and the while.* This is a long line. Probably *to him* counts as one stressed syllable, and *and the* as an unstressed one.

175   *like a fool.* Professional fools wore their hair and beard shaved.

176   *present* immediate

177   *conjuror.* See IV.4.45.

183   *scorch* (referring to the *brands of fire* of line 171)

185   *Guard with halberds.* The Duke calls on some of the *other officers* (line 129, stage direction) to be ready with their weapons. A *halberd* was a combination of spear and battle-axe, with a sharp blade ending in a point, and a spear-head, mounted on a shaft about six feet long. The display of force in this situation is likely to cause laughter, and indeed invites burlesque.

188   *housed* pursued (into a house)

192   *bestrid thee* stood ('strode') over you (in your defence). This is another piece of submerged narrative, rather like one that Shakespeare uses at a similar point of the action in *Twelfth Night* (V.1.49–56).

200   *in the strength and height of injury* in the most injurious manner possible

203   *Discover* show, reveal

205   *harlots.* The word could be applied to men as well as women, and was a less specific term of disapproval than at present, though Shakespeare generally uses it of sexual offenders.

208–9   *So befall my soul* | *As* let my soul's fate depend on whether

209   *burdens me withal* charges me with

210   *on night* at night

214   *advisèd* well aware of

216   *heady-rash provoked with* provoked to heady rashness by

219   *packed* in league

220   *witness* bear witness to

221   *parted* departed

226   *that gentleman* (the Merchant; IV.1)

227   *swear me down* swear in spite of my denial

231   *peasant* servant

233   *bespoke* asked

239   *anatomy* skeleton

240   *juggler*. The word had a range of meanings, generally 'entertainer', more specifically 'conjuror', 'sorcerer'.

241   *A needy, hollow-eyed, sharp-looking wretch*. This line is printed in F as 'A needy-hollow-ey'd-sharpe-looking-wretch;' which may be intended to indicate a gabbled delivery.

243   *took on him as* assumed the role of
        conjuror exorcist

245   *with no face ... outfacing me* (although he was so thin that he seemed to have no face, trying nevertheless to stare me out)

246   *possessed* mad

248   *dankish* dank, humid

263   *drew my sword*. See line 32.

269   *And this is false you burden me withal*. Antipholus echoes Adriana's accusation, line 209.

270   *impeach* charge, accusation

271   *Circe's cup* (the poisoned cup with which the sorceress Circe turned men to swine, in the *Odyssey*, Book X; the story is also told in Ovid's *Metamorphoses*. This is the climax of the transformation imagery in the play; see Introduction, pages 31–3.)

272   *housed*. See line 188 and Commentary.

273   *coldly* coolly, rationally

282   *mated* bewildered, confused
        mated, or stark mad. (At III.2.54, Antipholus of Syracuse claims that he is *Not mad, but mated*.)

283   EGEON. His almost entirely silent presence has given weight to the scene since his entrance at line 129. Now he steps forward.

288–91 *bondman ... bondman ... unbound*. This is spoken punningly, since Dromio is no longer tied up. It may also indicate that he has been given his freedom. In *Menaechmi* the visiting twin's bondsman is given his freedom in return for helping his master.

179

296   *look . . . strange on* pretend not to recognize
299   *careful* full of care
       deformèd ('deforming'; or perhaps part of a more
       positive personification, referring to the withered hand
       of Old Father Time)
300   *defeatures* disfigurement. (See II.1.98 and Commen-
       tary.)
302   *Neither* nor that either (after Antipholus's denial that
       he recognizes Egeon's appearance)
306   *bound* (punningly)
308   *extremity* extreme severity
310   *seven short years.* This is inconsistent with I.1.133,
       where Egeon says he has been travelling for only five
       years. This is probably accidental. It has been sug-
       gested that Shakespeare is here remembering the
       seven-year voyage of Aeneas in the *Aeneid* (V. K.
       Whitaker, *Shakespeare's Use of Learning* (1953), page
       85).
311   *my feeble key of untuned cares* the weak tone of my
       voice, altered by sorrow
312   *grainèd* furrowed, lined (like the grain of wood)
313   *sap-consuming winter's drizzled snow* the white hairs of
       youth-destroying age (his beard)
314   *conduits* channels, veins
       froze frozen
316   *lamps* (eyes)
321   *But* only
323   *shamest . . . misery.* Probably *shamest* has two syllables
       and *misery* two – 'mis'ry'.
331   (stage direction) The rather unusual stage direction is
       probably Shakespeare's, and suggests an intention that
       the wonder of the situation should be enhanced by the
       reactions of the spectators on the stage.
333   *genius* attendant spirit (supposed to accompany a man
       through life, and to resemble him identically). The
       word is italicized in F, which seems to suggest that it
       seemed foreign.

335   *deciphers* distinguishes
344   *at a burden* at one birth
345–52   Many editors move these lines to follow line 362, mainly on the grounds that the Abbess has not been *urging of her wrack at sea*. But neither does she do so in her next speech. Shakespeare permits a slight anomaly in the interests of economy.
348   *Antipholus'*. In Shakespeare, the plural of a word ending in 's' is often written and pronounced without the additional syllable.
349   *Dromios* (two syllables)
      semblance (three syllables) appearance
350–51   *sea – | These*. The syntax is confused. This may suggest textual dislocation, but more probably is intended to indicate the Duke's understandable bewilderment.
351   *children* (three syllables)
356–60   *By men of Epidamnum ... those of Epidamnum*. This corrects Egeon at I.1.112, where he says that his wife with one Antipholus and one Dromio was picked up *By fishermen of Corinth, as we thought*. Æmilia does not explain how she got from Epidamnum to Ephesus. Here, as elsewhere, Shakespeare's geography is impressionistic.
369   *Duke Menaphon* (not mentioned elsewhere in the play. The name occurs in Marlowe's *Tamburlaine*, written about 1587 and printed in 1590, and in Robert Greene's romance *Menaphon*, of 1589.)
376   *leisure* opportunity
379   *be* may be
387   *still* continually, repeatedly
389   *errors* (alluding to the play's title, as again at line 398)
      are arose have arisen
392   *diamond* (her ring: IV.3.69)
393   *cheer* entertainment
398   *sympathizèd* (in which we have all shared)
401   *Thirty-three years*. Earlier editors sometimes emended this inconsistency.

405   *calendars of their nativity* (the Dromios, because they mark the age of the Antipholuses)

406   *gossips' feast* a feast of godparents (at which all the characters will be symbolically re-baptized)

406-7 *go with me. | After so long grief, such nativity.* These lines have often been emended. *Go* is often altered to 'joy', and run on with the following line, so that it means 'and enjoy with me ... such a christening party.' This may be right, but *go with me* makes satisfactory sense, especially if taken as with an emphasis on *me* – an Abbess. *Nativity* itself has also been frequently emended, usually to either 'festivity' or 'felicity', because of objections to its repetition from the end of line 405. But *nativity* here maintains the imagery of birth begun in line 401, and it may even be, as C. J. Sisson suggested, in his *New Readings in Shakespeare* (1956), that the word (spelt both times with a capital in F) was intended to bear special significance at the Christmas performance of the play in 1594 (see page 10).

409   *stuff* baggage, belongings

411   *at host* at the hostel (inn)

416   *kitchened me* entertained me in the kitchen

418   *glass* mirror

420   *gossiping* merrymaking (especially of godparents at a christening party)

423.   *cuts* (straws of uneven length) lots

AN ACCOUNT OF THE TEXT

The Comedy of Errors was first printed in 1623, some thirty years after it was written, in the first Folio edition of Shakespeare's collected plays (referred to below as F). This is the only authoritative text of this play. There are many signs that the manuscript from which the printers worked was the author's own, which had not undergone the kind of regularization that would be likely to occur in the theatre in preparation for its use as a prompt copy. There are, for instance, inconsistencies among the speech headings such as would have had to be cleared up by the prompter. These are particularly confusing in references to the twins. For instance, Antipholus of Syracuse is named '*Antipholis Erotes*' when he first appears at the beginning of I.2 (see Commentary to I.2, opening stage direction), and the Ephesian Dromio is '*E. Dro.*' in speech headings. This means that '*E. Ant.*' signifies Antipholus of Syracuse but '*E. Dro.*', Dromio of Ephesus. The stage directions, too, seem to be the author's, as some of them provide information beyond what would have been needed for practical purposes by the prompter (for example, '*Enter Adriana, wife to Antipholis Sereptus*', II.1.0) and sometimes beyond what is supplied by the dialogue (for example, '*Enter . . . a Schoolemaster, call'd Pinch*', IV.4.37).

The action of *The Comedy of Errors* is continuous, with only a few brief time-gaps, and, although its structure may have been influenced by the five-act scheme of classical drama, Shakespeare is unlikely to have intended any breaks in performance. Clear evidence to the contrary is provided by the direction at V.1.9, which says: '*Enter Antipholus and Dromio againe*' (they had left the stage at the end of Act IV). In F the text is divided into five acts, though these are not subdivided into scenes. The act division was probably made by someone other than the author when the text was being prepared for printing. On the whole the play is well printed, though there are some obvious misprints, some mislineation, and a few passages where the text seems to be seriously corrupt (for example, II.1.107-13, III.2.49, and V.1.401-7). These last are discussed in the Commentary.

In this edition, spelling and punctuation of the text have been modernized in accordance with the principles of the series, speech prefixes have been made consistent, and stage directions have been regularized and amplified where necessary. Conventional act and scene divisions are indicated. The Collations that follow record departures from F; places where this edition preserves readings that are altered in some current editions; and the more important modifications of the original stage directions. Quotations from F are given in the original spelling, but long 's' (ſ) has been replaced by the modern form. The more interesting textual points are discussed in the Commentary.

COLLATIONS

I

Emendations

The following list indicates readings of this edition which depart from those of F. The reading to the left of the square bracket is that of this edition. (Stage directions are listed separately, below.) This list does not include corrections of obvious misprints. Alterations of punctuation are recorded when a decision affecting the sense has had to be made. Most of these emendations were first made by eighteenth-century editors. Those first made, unauthoritatively, in the second Folio (1632) or the third Folio (1663) are attributed to F2 or F3. A few recently suggested are attributed to the name of the scholar who first proposed them.

THE CHARACTERS IN THE PLAY] *not in* F

I.1. 16–17 Nay, more: | If any born at Ephesus be seen]
Nay more, if any borne at *Ephesus* | Be seene

42 Epidamnum] *Epidamium* (*and throughout, i.e. at*
I.1.63, I.2.1, IV.1.86 *and* 95, V.1.356 *and* 360)

61–3 soon | We came aboard. | A] soone wee came
aboord. | A

103 upon] vp

124 thee] they

152 health] (*J. Dover Wilson, 1922*); helpe

I.2. 40 In quest of them unhappy,] In quest of them
(vnhappie a)

66 clock] cooke

93 God's] (F3); God

II.1. 12 ill] thus

61 thousand] hundred

70–74 Quoth my master ... beat me there] *prose in* F

79–80 An ... beating, | Between] (*this edition*); And ...
beating: | Betweene

112 Wear] Where

113 But] By

II.2. 12 didst] did didst

46–51 Why ... for what] *prose in* F

86 men] them

106 tiring] trying

110 e'en] in

145 off] of

155 unstained] distain'd

184 stronger] stranger

195 offered] free'd

204 am not I] am I not

III.1. 54 trow] hope

89 her] your

91 her] your

110 yet, too, gentle] yet too gentle

III.2. 1 LUCIANA] *Iulia.*

4 building] buildings

III.2.   4 ruinous] ruinate
          21 but] not
          26 wife] (F2); wise
          46 sister's] sister
          49 bed] (F2); bud
          57 where] when
          75 art, Dromio. Thou] art *Dromio,* thou
        114 and] is
     153–4 And I think . . . i'the wheel] *prose in* F
       156 An if] And if
IV.1.   17 her] their
         88 then she] then sir she
IV.2.   6 Of] Oh,
     44–6 I know . . . his desk] *prose in* F
       48 That] (F2); Thus
       60 'a] I
IV.3.   60 if you do, expect] (F2); if do expect
     71–6 Some . . . it] *prose in* F
IV.4.   40 to prophesy] the prophesie
     111 his] (*S. Tannenbaum, 1932*); this
V.1.   33 God's] (F3); God
       46 much, much] (F2); much
       66 at] *not in* F
    235–6 By . . . more] *one line in* F
     403 ne'er] are
     423 senior] Signior

2

Rejected emendations

The following list gives readings of F which have been pre-
served in this edition but which are emended in some current
editions. It does not attempt to record once-accepted emendations that are now generally rejected. The reading of the present
edition, following F, is given to the left of the square bracket.

The exact reading of F is given, in round brackets, to the right of the square bracket when this seems necessary to illustrate how ambiguity of interpretation might arise. Then come the proposed emendations, separated by semi-colons when there are more than one. Many of these emendations were first made by eighteenth-century editors, but some are modern. The more interesting ones are discussed in the Commentary.

I.1. 16–18 Nay, more: | If any born at Ephesus be seen | At any Syracusian] Nay more: if any born at Ephesus | Be seen at Syracusian

39 me, had] me too, had (F2)

40 joy, our] joy; our

55 mean woman] meaner woman; poor mean woman

56 burden male, twins both] burden, male twins, both

76 none –] (this it was: (for other meanes was none) | The Sailors . . . F); none:

128 so] for

152 To seek thy health by beneficial help] (To seeke thy helpe by beneficiall helpe, F); To seek thy help by beneficial hap; To seek thy hope by beneficial help; To seek thy life by beneficial help; To seek thy pelf by beneficial help

156 Gaoler, take] Gaoler, go take

I.2. 40 them unhappy,] them unhappier

65 scour] score

II.1. 20–21 Man . . . master . . . | Lord] Men . . . masters | Lords

39 would] wouldst

68 I know not thy mistress] I know thy mistress not

107 alone a love] (alone, a loue F); alone alone; alone o'love; alone a toy

110 Yet the] that the; and though

111 and] yet

II.2.   3–4   out ... report.] out. .... report

          95   jollity] policy

    110–11   e'en no time] (in no time F); no time (F2)

   117–18   I ... yonder] *as verse*

      150   crime] grime

   154–5   Keep then ... thou undishonourèd] I live distained, thou undishonourèd. | Keep then fair league and truce with thy true bed

      199   We talk with goblins, owls, and sprites] We talk with fairies, goblins, elves, and sprites; We talk with none but goblins, elves and sprites

      203   thou Dromio] thou drone

III.1.   47   face] office

             a name] an aim

       65   in pain] in, i'faith

       71   cake here] cake there

     106   ever] e'er

     108   mirth] wrath

III.2.   2   Antipholus,] Antipholus, hate

       20   deeds] deed

             is] are

       49   thee] them

       66   I am thee] I aim thee

     107   kept. For why? She] (kept: for why? she F); kept, for why she

   141–2   o'er embellished] o'er-embellished

IV.1.   56   me by] by me

       99   end as] end, sir, as

IV.2.   2   austerely] a surety

       29   sweet] sweat

       33   him,] him by the heel

       35   fairy] fury

       46   him, mistress, redemption] him, Mistress Redemption,

       60   'a] (I F); he; Time

IV.3.   13   What, have you got] Where have you got

       35   ships] ship (F2)

	51–2	Nay . . . dam] *as a verse line (See Commentary.)*
	54	as much to say] as much as to say
	65	then] thou
IV.4.	28	ears] years
	150	saw] see
V.1.	12	to me] with me
	26	thee] thee swear it
	79	moody and dull] moody, heavy, and dull
	183	scorch] scotch
	347–52	Why . . . together] *moved to follow line* 362
	406	go] joy
	407	nativity] festivity; felicity

3

Stage directions

The stage directions of this edition are based on those of F. The original directions have been normalized and clarified when necessary, and some further directions have been added to indicate necessary action. All directions for speeches to be given aside or addressed to a particular character are editorial. Below are listed some of the other additions and alterations to F's directions. Minor alterations such as the addition of a character's name to *Exit*, the normalization of characters' names, and the provision of exits and entrances where they are obviously demanded by the context are not listed.

I.2.	0	*First Merchant*] *a Marchant*
	92	*not in* F
II.1.	81	*not in* F
	85	*not in* F
III.1.	64	*not in* F
III.2.	0	*Luciana*] *Iuliana (See Commentary.)*
IV.1.	0	*Second Merchant*] *a Merchant*
IV.2.	61	*with the money*] *not in* F

IV.4.   0   *with the Officer] with a Iailor*

         17   *not in* F

         51   *not in* F

       104   *after line* 103 *in* F

       111   *not in* F

       128   *Exeunt Pinch and his assistants carrying off Antipholus of Ephesus and Dromio of Ephesus. The Officer, Adriana, Luciana, and the Courtesan remain] Exeunt. Manet Offic. Adri. Luci. Courtizan (after line* 129)

       141   *Enter Antipholus of Syracuse and Dromio of Syracuse, with their rapiers drawn] Enter Antipholus Siracusia with his Rapier drawne, and Dromio Sirac.*

       144   *(see Commentary)*

V.1.   0   *Second Merchant] the Merchant*

MORE ABOUT PENGUINS
AND PELICANS

For further information about books available from Penguins please write to Dept EP, Penguin Books Ltd, Harmondsworth, Middlesex UB7 0DA.

In the U.S.A.: For a complete list of books available from Penguins in the United States write to Dept CS, Penguin Books, 625 Madison Avenue, New York, New York 10022.

In Canada: For a complete list of books available from Penguins in Canada write to Penguin Books Canada Ltd, 2801 John Street, Markham, Ontario L3R 1B4.

In Australia: For a complete list of books available from Penguins in Australia write to the Marketing Department, Penguin Books Australia Ltd, P.O. Box 257, Ringwood, Victoria 3134.

NEW PENGUIN SHAKESPEARE
General Editor: T. J. B. Spencer

All's Well That Ends Well Barbara Everett
Antony and Cleopatra Emrys Jones
As You Like It H. J. Oliver
Coriolanus G. R. Hibbard
Hamlet T. J. B. Spencer
Henry IV, Part 1 P. H. Davison
Henry IV, Part 2 P. H. Davison
Henry V A. R. Humphreys
Henry VI, Part 1 Norman Sanders
Henry VI, Part 2 Norman Sanders
Henry VI, Part 3 Norman Sanders
Henry VIII A. R. Humphreys
Julius Caesar Norman Sanders
King John R. L. Smallwood
King Lear G. K. Hunter
Macbeth G. K. Hunter
Measure for Measure J. M. Nosworthy
The Merchant of Venice W. Moelwyn Merchant
The Merry Wives of Windsor G. R. Hibbard
A Midsummer Night's Dream Stanley Wells
Much Ado About Nothing R. A. Foakes
Othello Kenneth Muir
Pericles Philip Edwards
The Rape of Lucrece J. W. Lever
Richard II Stanley Wells
Richard III E. A. J. Honigmann
Romeo and Juliet T. J. B. Spencer
The Taming of the Shrew G. R. Hibbard
The Tempest Anne Righter (Anne Barton)
Timon of Athens G. R. Hibbard
Twelfth Night M. M. Mahood
The Two Gentlemen of Verona Norman Sanders
The Two Noble Kinsmen N. W. Bawcutt
The Winter's Tale Ernest Schanzer